Faking it with Archie
A rent-a-date story

Danielle Jacks

Faking it with Archie © 2022 Danielle Jacks

The Faking it with Archie is written in British English. This book is the work of fiction. Any names, characters, places, and events are either creations of the author's imagination or used fictitiously. Any similarities are purely coincidental.

Copyright © 2022 by Danielle Jacks.

All rights are reserved. Published in the United Kingdom by Danielle Jacks.

No part of this book may be used or reproduced without the author's written consent, except in the case of a brief quotation to enhance reviews or articles.

Editor: Karen Sanders

Proofreader: Mich Feeney

Faking it with Archie

Faking it with Archie
A rent-a-date story

Blurb

Victoria Ainsworth is a name I'm hoping to get in to every high street store. I'm one of Rebel Jacks' top designers and fashion is my life. When Archibald Banks auditions for a modelling job with me, we get off to a shaky start. He's drop-dead gorgeous and I judge him all wrong. When I'm given the opportunity to attend a high-profile ball, I need a date, but there's a catch; Archibald Banks is the only man for the job. Thanks to a picture of the two of us on social media, my mother thinks we're dating. Can I advance my career and fake date a guy who might be more irresistible than I first thought?

CHAPTER ONE

I look at the two male models in front of me. One has a street model look that is too cool. He's a hipster type. You know, the dark, sexy eyes and a lickable abdominal V. He'd rock a beanie and get the girl, even if his vocabulary was made up of one-word sentences. *Sup… Vibe…* you get the idea. The other guy is his complete opposite. He looks like he belongs in the church choir next to my Aunt Margorie, singing songs made for angels rather than at a modelling audition. The Christmas cardigan I've designed paired with burgundy jeans suits them both, and I have to choose which guy is most likely to sell the goods.

"What are you thinking, Victoria?" Melanie, my assistant says as she comes to stand next to me. She has her clipboard poised, ready to write down the name of the model I'm choosing to showcase my design to my boss, Jake.

I've worked for Rebel Jacks for almost five years, and

fashion is my life. The label is 'urban-chic style for the modern person without breaking the bank'. After graduating from the London School of Design, I worked my ass off to get this job, and I'd like my own full line of clothing by the end of next year. At twenty-six, I'm one of the youngest top designers at the company, and I take my coffee with a huge spoonful of ambition.

"If I want this to be a gift for unexpecting sons, I should go with choir boy, but if I want to sell it to the twenty to thirty-year-old man, I should go with Mr Abs," I say, waving my finger between them.

"If you put a shirt over those toned muscles, *he* might be boyfriend material." I wasn't aware Melanie was looking for a boyfriend for someone. I hope it's not me. She pushes her glasses up to get a closer look. I pull a decorative handkerchief from my top pocket and pretend to wipe the imaginary drool from her mouth. She swats my hand away. We stare at each other for a few seconds while I try to compose myself. She licks her lips in a lusty way, making us both laugh. I shake out my hands, trying to get my professional head back on. We then focus back on the two guys.

The tall, dark, and lickable one is the most attractive and my usual type. "No. He's a guaranteed heartbreaker," I mumble. He's staring at me with his brown, brooding eyes, but unless he can lip-read or read my mind, my thoughts are safe.

I haven't dated in years because I want a career more than a relationship. I'll do anything to get my designs in the right places, but the guy reminds me of my school boyfriend. Not in the way he looks. Just too good-looking to be faithful. I wrinkle my nose at the memory of Benedict Robinson. He was my first love and my first experience of betrayal.

I shake my head. I am *not* here looking for a suitable partner. I'm not even trying to arrange a one-night stand. This is work, and Christmas is about love, not lust. That's what I'm aiming for with my cardigan.

"Where did you just go?" Melanie asks.

I've been staring at the guy shamelessly, and it has nothing to do with clothing. "Sorry. I'm ready for a coffee. Hire the choir boy and let's get to the canteen." Melanie usually brings our drinks to my desk, but I need a change of scenery.

"Are you sure?" She pouts, making it clear she would've picked the other guy.

"Yes. I'll grab my bag and meet you at the lift in five." I go to my office to get my things, and Melanie approaches the models to give them the news.

I check my light brown hair in the mirror I keep in my desk drawer and rub at my blue eyes. I look tired, and I dab some concealer onto my dark circles. My late nights designing is showing.

I wait outside the lift for Melanie to finish up. The office is full of chatter as people go about their jobs. I check my emails on my phone while I wait.

"Ms. Ainsworth, please can I have some feedback on

today's casting call?" tall, dark, and sinful says. He sounds different from what I expected. He's polite and doesn't seem to have the arrogance about him that I'd anticipated. I glance behind him, but there's no sign of Melanie to save me. If I'd paid more attention, I'd know his name instead of having to describe him by his best qualities in my head.

"Thank you for coming to the audition. I'm sorry you didn't get the job."

"Why is that?" he asks, crossing his arms over his chest. He's wearing his own clothes now. A plain blue t-shirt and jeans. My cardigan would finish his outfit off perfectly.

"You're handsome, however, the other guy had the look I was aiming for with this design." The lift arrives, and a group of my co-workers get out.

"The label's called Rebel Jacks. The guy you've hired, Lloyd, looks more like a saint."

He has some balls to question my choices, especially when he's trying to convince me to change my mind. His initially good nature is slipping away.

"Aren't you ready to leave and go to your next casting call?" I ask, gesturing to the lift which will help him get out of here. I'm not trying to be rude, it's just I doubt he'd be happy with any of my excuses, and telling him I judged him as a jackass probably won't help the situation.

"No." He shakes his head.

"Okay, well, I'm in need of a coffee. Better luck next time." I think I'm leaving him on the third floor, but he follows me inside the lift.

"I'm not done with this conversation. I worked hard to get this meeting with you. I shaved off my stubble as I know you like your guys clean-cut, and I styled my hair using inspiration from your previous models. I'm perfect for Rebel Jacks, and I adjusted for you."

If he wants an A, he can have it for effort, although he's a little full-on. This guy seems to know more about me than I know about myself. He's enthusiastic, but I've made my decision.

I press the button for the ground floor. The quicker I get my coffee, the sooner I'll get rid of him. "I can see you take pride in your appearance, and I can appreciate that." That sounded like something I'd memorised for an interview. What does he want me to say, though? *'You're good enough for a one-night stand, but not to bring my cardigan home to a girl's parents?'*

The doors shut, making me feel trapped. I breathe in and out slowly, hoping the journey will pass quickly.

"All I need is a shot to prove I'm right for you." He glares intently at me. It's unsettling, but kind of alluring. He's wrong for the label. He should cut his losses and head home.

He's completely perfect for the label. It's me he's wrong for.

I need to find a way to make him go away which doesn't end with me being called a cold-hearted bitch. "If you give me your card, I'll put it in my personal file. If something comes up, I'll give you a call." I'm hoping by taking his business details, I'm giving him enough hope to move on.

"Your office has my phone number." He frowns. Maybe he's suspicious I'm not being genuine.

"Yes, but not many guys make it into my personal file."

Did I really just say that? I could slap myself. Quickly, I pull the corners of my mouth up into a strangled smile. After a few seconds, he hands me a card from his wallet. It reads, *Archibald Banks model, rent-a-date, and personal chef.* Underneath is his number and email address.

"Thank you." He starts to say something more, but the doors open to the ground floor, and I make a hasty exit into the staff canteen. I don't look back, and he can't follow me in here without a lanyard.

I order a black coffee before finding an empty seat. I send Melanie a text so she knows where I've gone, then I finish checking my emails and sip my coffee.

"Sorry, I got held up with Lloyd." Melanie places her bag on the table before getting herself a drink.

"Archibald Banks doesn't like to be told no," I say, rubbing my forehead when she returns.

"You've learned his name. Interesting." She gives me a knowing look.

"He collared me outside the lift, and I was forced to

deal with him. His name was collateral for getting him to leave." I wave the card at her that hasn't made it into my purse yet.

"You should've chosen Archie; Lloyd is high maintenance." She frowns, which is code for, *ask me about it, I dare you.*

"What happened after I left?"

Once we get the perfect picture with Lloyd, I'll only have to meet with him a handful of times. Other than seeing his face in my favourite fashion magazine, Gallant, I'll be able to delegate my commitments to Melanie. The picture is going to be the lead in my winter campaign and I want it to be perfect.

"He wanted an advance on his fee and a driver to pick him up for the official shoot. Even I have to catch the train to Rebel Jacks. He's only working for a day." She sips her tea, rolling her eyes.

I'm lucky to have a flat in Knighten Street, near the Thames, which isn't too far from the office. I walk the short distance most days, but I have a driver if I need one. "What did you tell him?"

"I told him we'd be in touch."

I narrow my eyes. Something's not right. "Before or after he signed the contract?"

She takes a long drink, pausing to add dramatic effect. "Before."

I take a drink. I've been given the opportunity to

change my mind on my model choice, and Archibald seems enthusiastic. Yet something is holding me back. "I'm going to sleep on it and reassess."

She has that look in her eye like she's thinking up a plan. I love my assistant, but she can be devilish.

We finish our break and go back to the office. Melanie takes her seat at her desk, and I close the door to my room. There's a pack of Christmas cards on my desk, and when I see the robin, I groan. My assistant is already thinking ahead and organising my business obligations. Christmas isn't my favourite time of year. The autumn leaves are still falling from the trees and the festivities are months away. If I sign these now, Melanie won't have to chase me for them later and she can tick them off her list of things to do, but I can't bring myself to open them. I push the packet to one side. The only thing I'm looking forward to is the winter wardrobe. My parents usually holiday in the Bahamas where it's warm, and my brother spends it with his friends.

Since I chose a career over getting married young, my relationship with my parents has been strained. Alexander Huntington the third was the man they picked out for me. He's old money like me, and a good match. However, the idea of marrying him makes me nauseous even now. Instead of enjoying fashion, I'd be expected to run a house and plan parties. I wouldn't be my true self. My father hasn't spoken to me much since I went against his wishes, and it hurts, but I won't change my mind on how to live my life.

I won't be with my family at Christmas. Instead, I'll be alone in my apartment as usual. It'll be like a normal day, only with a speech from the King.

I open up my design board and sketch out a spring dress. It's not even September and I'm ready to skip the festivities.

CHAPTER TWO

It's the day of the big photo shoot, and I'm meeting the crew at Lapland UK to get the final pictures. They've already started preparing their handmade winter wonderland, and Melanie says it's the perfect place to get my full-page spread for Gallant.

My driver will be here soon to take me on the hour-plus journey to Ascot. I'm wearing one of my handmade autumn dresses, and I've paired it with a Zosie handbag. One of my friends from the London School of Design, Morgan, is the founder of the accessory company, and I'm happy to support her brand. After applying my perfume and pink blush lipstick, I hurry to the car.

Once at the location, I can see why Melanie has chosen this place. It's perfect.

"Good morning," she says, handing me one of the coffee cups in her hand. She crosses the courtyard and I follow her into one of the barns.

"You've done an excellent job finding such a great backdrop." The smell of fern and cinnamon assaults my nostrils.

"I'd never let you down." She smiles. The candy cane door frames and Christmas décor is absolutely amazing. It warms even my anti-festive heart.

"So, where is Lloyd?" After re-thinking my decision, I told her to hire him anyway.

"Our model's in the toy workshop, which is just this way." She leads me through the barn, past the reindeer, and into an authentic-looking craft station.

"Did you bring my cardigan?"

"Of course."

We find most of the crew chatting away in the workshop. There's a workbench set-up in the centre of the room, and it looks perfect for the picture. I love seeing my designs come to life, and this one's extra special as it's the forefront of my whole winter collection.

A shirtless man approaches me, and I struggle to lift my eyes up to his face. Once I meet his gaze, I try not to react.

"Thank you, Victoria, for reconsidering me," Archie says, and my bottom lip drops a little. His chiselled jawline and mesmerising dark eyes temporarily short circuit my brain. Melanie clearly decided to go against my wishes and hired him. I give her a stern look, hoping she knows we'll be talking about this.

"Sure. Are you ready to impress?" I ask. He's already made my mouth water and he hasn't even done anything yet. It should be a crime to be that good-looking. I need to try and act normal so we can get through this day without any hitches.

"I won't let you down." His smile looks sincere, and I believe him.

I take my seat next to Melanie while the photographer sets up. "Did you get their numbers mixed up?" I ask, knowing full well she tricked me.

"If I had worn a lounge suit when they were apparently fashionable, you'd have corrected my error. Nobody wants to be reminded of that disaster. I'm merely returning the favour." She shrugs, but I don't miss the twitch of her bottom lip. She's anxious about my reaction.

I want to put her mind at ease because she's probably judged this situation better than I did. "Good call."

She sighs with relief. I don't think I'm a stern boss, but going behind my back was a bold move. It was also the correct thing to do. My cardigan wears him well. The photographer gets a range of pictures, including some fun ones of him working in the toy factory. After a couple of hours, I send everyone for a break while I look through the pictures on my laptop. Archibald Banks has done a great job, and any of these pictures would be perfect. I send a selfie of myself with the Zosie bag and Archie's pictures in the background to Morgan. Underneath I write: **Hard day out of the office.**

Morgan replies: **Yummy. I bet you're loving him. I wish I could borrow him to help me with these new satchels.** She sends a picture of a silver fox wearing a beautiful watch, and her bag is on a table in front of him next to a coffee cup.

Why aren't you using a younger model?

The satchels might be expensive, but my budget isn't. The guy in the picture is someone's grandpa and he works for free.

I laugh. **You can't argue with free.**

"What's so funny?" Archie asks, startling me.

I clutch my hand to my chest. "I didn't realise I had company. Everyone has another ten minutes break. Why are you back so early?"

"I wanted to check you were liking my work." He pushes his hair back away from his face.

I lean back on the table next to the laptop. "Yes. I think we're going to be finished early today."

He moves closer to me so he can take a look. He smells amazing, and the proximity is messing with my head. "Would you consider doing a little extra modelling? I have a friend who needs some help. She can't pay you much, but you'd get exposure, and I'll give you a copy of all the photos for your portfolio."

"When?" He rubs his chin while thinking about my offer.

"I need to check with her, but we could head over

there once we've finished here."

"Okay." He grins, and I find myself returning his smile. He's so determined when he wants something, yet he doesn't give anything away when he doesn't have to.

I read Morgan's message: **You have to fake it until you make it, even when it comes to models.**

How would you like Archie and me to stop by on our way back to London? He might be able help you out for an hour or two?

For real?

Yup. I grin, glad I can help her out.

Awesome.

We finish up at the Christmas wonderland, and I inform my driver to make the extra stop. I take the cardigan with me and send the crew, including my assistant, home.

"Did you have fun today?" I ask Archie.

"Yes, thank you. I hope you're pleased with the photos."

"Very. Melanie made the right choice with you." I nod, glad he will be the one in the magazines. He was easy to work with.

He frowns. "I thought you changed your mind."

Oops. I forgot how much my approval meant to him.

I could tell him the truth, but I decide to bend it slightly. "It was with her guidance, shall we say."

We make small talk while on our journey. He seems down to earth and nothing like my first impression of him. If anything, he seems like the sort of guy I'd meet and he'd already have a girlfriend. He's a catch.

Morgan's outside when we reach her studio. She has her camera around her neck and is taking pictures of jewellery amongst her flowerbeds. She's good at improvising, and I miss seeing her every day like when we studied together.

"Hello, handsome," she says to Archie when we step out of the car.

He gives her a wicked smile I've not seen before. His whole face lights up as he goes over to introduce himself. I either rub him up the wrong way or make him too serious. It shouldn't bother me that he's professional with me, but it does. I find it hard to relax, especially when it comes to work. I'm focused and driven, but I'd like to see the sexy smiles too.

"I'm honoured you'd consider using me, "Archie tells Morgan.

"The pleasure is mine." She winks at him, and I try not to frown. I wish she wouldn't flirt with every good-looking guy she meets. "Welcome. Come inside." They begin to look through some of her jewellery. "Bring your cardigan. I won't release the pictures until your grand debut."

I do as she asks, and when I get inside, she's showing

Archie a collection of satchels. He tries them on, and she takes a few snaps.

"Shall I make coffee?" I ask, pointing to the small kitchen.

"No, get over here," Morgan says. She tugs me over to Archie. "I want the two hottest people I know to pose with my latest collection."

"I'm a designer, not a model." I shake my head in protest.

"Remember my shoestring budget." She pouts.

"Fine. What do you want me to do?" She switches my bag for a new one and pulls out my hair tie. She combs through my hair and clips in a hair extension. Once she gives me earrings, a necklace, and a bracelet, I stand next to Archie, who has removed his shirt. I try not to blush as he places his hand on my waist.

"Don't stand like you're doing a police line-up. Relax and have fun." She puts my arm across his shoulder. My hair is tucked behind one ear, and she positions me to face him. "Look at his jawline, not his chest."

I glare at her, and Archie's ribs shake with laughter.

After the first few pictures, I start to get into it. I put on a few different bags and matching accessories. We pose, and I enjoy myself, but the time passes quickly, and we have to say our goodbyes.

Archie and I walk back to the car.

"Is every day in your life like this?" Archie asks.

"I wish. This was so much fun," I say, opening the passenger door.

"Yes, it was." He smiles, and it lights up his whole face. That's the kind of look I want to see. We get into the vehicle and the driver sets off.

"My job is pretty cool, though. I adore what I do." That's the truth. Seeing people in my clothes is the best feeling in the world.

"I can imagine it is. You get to dress up and change things you don't like. Do you play catwalk in your office? I bet you and your assistant love it." He pretends to strut his stuff.

I laugh. He's close to the truth. I have Melanie modelling most of my designs while trying not to get stabbed by the sewing pins. "Only sometimes. Don't tell anyone, though."

He holds up his hand in scout's honour. "Your secret's safe with me." He winks as he lowers his arm. There's something about Archie that brings out my playful side. I could tell him about my toy fashion studio and he wouldn't judge me.

My driver takes Archie to the train station, and I wish the journey had taken longer.

"Goodbye," he says as he gets out of the car.

"Goodbye." I watch him walk away. His ass looks great in his tight trousers, and I don't take my eyes off him until he's out of sight.

We continue through London and the driver takes me home. Once alone, I sit on the sofa with a glass of wine, reflecting on my day. It's quiet, and usually I'd find it peaceful in my apartment, but tonight, I just feel alone.

CHAPTER THREE

"It's finally here," Melanie says, shaking the copy of Gallant. Her voice is so high-pitched; I'd laugh if I wasn't so nervous.

My stomach churns. I hope it's good. "Have you already looked?" I ask, reaching for it over my desk. The suspense is killing me, and I want to rip the magazine wide open.

She pouts her lips in the way she does when she's outraged at my words. "No. I wanted to see your face when you see our gorgeous man." Her expression turns into an over-eager smile.

"Did you send him a copy?" I flick through the pages, looking for our advert while trying to play it cool. I'm as excited as Melanie, I'm just better at hiding it.

"Of course I did, and I sent one to Jake." She makes imaginary ticks in the air like she's mentally marking them off on her list.

"Let's hope he doesn't use it as a coaster this time." I roll my eyes and we both laugh.

My boss is a lover of fashion, but not magazines. If he saw a Rebel Jacks design, he'd want an A1 poster for the building, but he won't look for small adverts unless they're pointed out to him. Finally, I get a glimpse of our winter wonderland as I turn the next page.

"Wow. It's beautiful." The wooden buttons and vibrant cashmere look divine against Archibald's tight abs. I'd forgotten how handsome he was until seeing this. The photoshoot was about a month ago, but it feels like longer.

"I have a good feeling about this." Melanie circles the buttons like she's really touching them.

"Me too. Tonight, we should celebrate. Drinks and food at Late Bites, on me?" It's been a while since we did anything other than work, and it would be nice to go out.

"That sounds perfect. Shall I book the table?" She pulls out her phone and starts typing.

"Yes."

She goes back to her desk, and I work on my spring collection. I spend a couple of hours sketching and cutting out small samples of fabric. Melanie brings me a couple of cups of tea to keep me hydrated while I stay lost in my work.

"Have you seen this?" she asks when she brings me a

refill. The work tablet is under her arm, and she waves it in front of me.

I tuck my pencil behind my ear as she places the cup on my drawing station. "What do you have to show me?"

"Your cardigan is trending on TikTok." She presses play on a video of a woman dressed in my cashmere and her bra. The background is a blue photo prop screen. She wears her clothing with pride. Archie's picture is in her hand with #anti-boyfriend written in marker pen across his face. She tears it up and blows a kiss as it falls to the ground. The next clip is similar, only she's also wearing one of Morgan's necklaces. Lots of women have made these TikToks, calling it the only boyfriend a girl needs for Christmas. The beautiful picture of Archie is being rubbished all over the U.K.

I'm shocked at first, then guilt washes over me. That's Archie being ripped apart. My mouth is hanging open. My big ad campaign is getting torn up.

But… to make the videos, they are purchasing my cardigan, and it seems like it's the model they are dissing. I watch more TikToks. These women are all wearing my design and making it look hot. My spread in Gallant might've worked in an unconventional way.

"This is good, right? How many cardigans have we sold?" My winter collection has only been live for a week and has only just hit the general press. It's hard to explain the feeling I get when someone is enjoying my hard work.

Melanie takes the tablet and goes to the Rebel Jacks website. "No way."

"What?"

She turns the screen to show a red *sold out* banner. Excitement bubbles in my stomach. This has never happened to me before.

"I need to check the data." We go to her desk, and she uploads the selling page. "You've sold 10,500 cardigans! I knew this was going to be your year. This is awesome. We need to go see the boss to see if he'll commission some more cardigans while it's hot."

We clasp hands in excitement, and I can't help grinning. I've waited for this moment all my life. It feels like I just won an award, and maybe I have with the *sold out* banner. We don't have to make our way up to the top floor because Jake is heading our way when we look out of the doorway.

"Great job, Victoria. It looks like you'll be making snowstorms this winter," Jake quips. He's wearing a thick jumper and jeans. The weather reference fits well with his outfit. Looking at him, you'd think it was cold in here, but it's not. He's going soft in his old age, but a compliment from him is a big deal because he doesn't give them out often. Recognition for my work is all I've ever wanted.

"Thank you."

"Get your assistant to find a female model and we'll reshoot the campaign."

Words get stuck in my throat and my smile freezes. Archie's disapproving face flashes across my mind. "Have you seen Gallant? The guy I picked was amazing."

"That's not what the people want." He shakes his head.

"But…"

He waves off my objection. "I want the new pictures on my desk tomorrow."

The first campaign took weeks to organise, and now he wants me to re-do it overnight. He doesn't give me a chance to say anything more as he goes into a meeting at the end of the hall.

"I can see where he's coming from. Women being empowered is what's selling, but we can kiss goodbye to the plans at Late Bites," I say to Melanie.

"It's almost the end of October. We can't use the Lapland set as it will be full of workers preparing for Santa's visit. We'll have to use whoever's free in the photography lab, and I'm not sure who can model for us."

I take a deep breath. We need positive vibes. "We've done a tight campaign before. I have the best assistant in the office, and I have faith this will be a success. We can pull it off. While we're being optimistic, reschedule our table for a later time."

"I'm already on it. First, I'll make the phone call, then we'll go find a photographer. Finding a model is the tricky part. Do you think we can find someone?"

"It's a hot campaign. I'm sure someone will snap it up." I cross my fingers.

Once we've agreed on the plan, we go down to find a photographer, and Malcolm offers to help. Luckily for us, he's been working on a Christmas film and has the perfect fireplace for the shoot. Melanie disappears to use her phone and we arrange to meet in a couple of hours on the movie set.

The time passes quickly as I pick out the perfect clothing and accessories to go with my cardigan. I arrive at the photoshoot a few minutes late. Melanie's already waiting with a blonde-haired woman.

"This is Victoria. Meet TikTok influencer, Fresh Rose," Melanie says when I make it to the fireplace. I recognise the young lady from the video earlier. Getting Rose here this quickly is impressive, even for my assistant. After formal greetings and signing paperwork, we get ready to take the pictures. I dress her in a black lacy halterneck dress and black stilettoes. I've chosen a long sparkly chain and a few black rose rings. The quality is classier than her Tik Tok videos, but still sexy. Rose does her own make-up, and Malcolm captures some great images. She's a natural poser and the camera loves her. We manage to get the proofs on Jake's desk and leave the office at nine. Someone must've been rooting for us today because it feels almost like a miracle.

Late Bites is busy by the time we step inside. The smell of fresh Italian bread makes my stomach growl.

Melanie gestures to the host and he clicks his fingers. A waitress shows us to our table against the back wall. It's been a while since we came out after work.

"Two glasses of prosecco, please," I say to the waitress.

"Coming right up," she says. She hands us some menus and goes to the bar to put in our order.

"What a crazy day," I say to Melanie, allowing myself to relax into the chair.

"Yes, but we pulled it off." She claps her hands together.

I'm excited but exhausted. I'm not sure where she gets her energy from.

The waitress puts the drinks on the table.

I pick my glass up. "Cheers."

"Cheers." We clink them together and complete the toast.

It's been a great day for business. Hopefully, tomorrow, Jake will approve more orders and I'll be Rebel Jacks' top designer of the year. This is definitely worth celebrating. I could get a promotion or be allowed a bigger collection.

"Would you ladies like to order food?" I turn, surprised to see Archie wearing a waiter's uniform.

"What are you doing here?" I ask, unable to hide my shock. The pitch of my voice is off, and my words seem unsure. A stab of culpability runs through me.

"I wish I could be a full-time model, but waiting tables is what pays the bills." He smiles easily.

"Did you get the magazine I sent you?" Melanie asks, smiling, but it's forced. The dismayed feeling in my stomach worsens.

"Yes. Thank you. I'm honoured to be featured in the ad." He stands tall, flexing his arms with pride.

I adjust my position in my chair. I'm uncomfortable about what we did today. From tomorrow morning, my cardigan is going to be all over London's billboards without him in it. I never made a promise to give him exclusivity, but it feels like a betrayal. "You're welcome. It was nice to work with you. Can we get two Caesar salads?" I say with a tight smile. I can't tell him happened. Partly because I'm a coward, but also because I don't want him to react badly in front of all these people.

"Yes. Coming right up." He notes down the order and collects the menus.

"Did you know he worked here?" I frown once he's left.

"No. I swear." Melanie holds her hands up. She looks as guilty as I feel.

In fashion, nobody gets anywhere without stepping on a few toes, and technically, I didn't do anything wrong. I try my best to enjoy the evening and forget about the sexiest pair of eyes in the room, but my gut is lined with guilt.

CHAPTER FOUR

A week later, my clothing is selling out as soon as it comes into stock. It's not just the cardigan; the whole collection is flying off the shelves. Some of my spring designs are in the workshop being turned into prototypes too. Everything is going so well that I have to keep pinching myself to make sure I'm awake.

"What do you think?" I ask Melanie as she brings me my coffee. She looks at the pencil skirt I've been perfecting for the last couple of days.

"Are you sure about the daisies?" She leans in.

"That's what's coming into fashion." I turn to look at her.

"Yes, but I don't think we need to see them on ladies' crotches."

I study the picture. "Move them over to the left?"

She tilts her head from side to side. "Maybe," she says, then leaves the room.

I nod. "I can fix this." Picking up a rubber, I erase the flowers and start again. I'm almost done when I hear loud voices outside my office.

"You can't go in there," Melanie shouts. I don't have long to wait to find out who my intruder is. Archie marches into my office with my assistant following close behind. "Sorry. I couldn't stop him."

He takes a seat and we both look at Melanie. "It's okay. I can handle this," I say, and she leaves us to talk. Once the door shuts, I sit behind my desk, staring at my visitor. "What can I do for you?"

"You fucked me over." He throws his hand up in the air.

"If we'd had sex, I'd know." That was my bad attempt at a joke, and I instantly regret it.

"That's not what I meant and you know it." He shakes his head.

"You got the Gallant spread. That's what we agreed on."

"I'm written as the boyfriend women don't need." He throws his hands in the air again.

"Bad publicity is better than no publicity." I cringe at my words. This line is usually used to help celebs feel better about a scandal, but I doubt it works.

"What's worse is everyone was talking about me

behind my back and nobody had the guts to tell me. I'm not on TikTok, so I didn't see the trend. I thought it was weird I was getting strange looks in the street. This is your fault." He forcefully taps my desk, and I'm wondering if he's imagining he's squashing me like a bug.

I understand his anger, but I'm not sure what I'm supposed to do. I thought his campaign would be forgotten about quickly anyway once the festive season was over. No one thinks about an outfit they saw in last year's magazines. However, Archie didn't get a fair shot, and I feel bad, even though it wasn't my fault.

"I didn't start the TikTok videos." Lack of confidence rings through my statement.

"Oh, so you didn't arrange for Rose to come into the studio so you could replace my ad and use her all over London? I saw three billboards this morning which should be mine." He pokes his chest.

While I understand his frustration, he has to know as well as I do that the fashion industry has never been fair. It's everyone for themselves, and while I don't love that fact, it's the truth.

"I gave my boss what he wanted. That's what happens when you want to do well at your job," I tell him. He stands, and I copy, leaning on my desk. I couldn't have gone against Jake's wishes, especially not without a better plan. I can't compete with an organic source like the TikTok trend. Those women love my design.

"When you gave me the callback, I thought we were on the same page."

"Melanie hired you!" I snap. That was the wrong thing to say, but it's not like I'm enjoying his misfortune. I'm a good person. My intention wasn't to hurt him, it was to succeed in a tough industry.

He moves close to my face. "You were the one who made me feel like you believed in me. You took me to your friend's workshop. I helped you out and you ditched my photo as soon as something better came along."

"I'm sorry you feel I've not given you the attention you needed. You got paid for the job you were contracted to do. The rest of it was out of my hands. If it makes you feel better, I'll ask my boss to release a few of Morgan's pictures on the website. I'll also update my personal photos to include you." I'm shouting, even though he's standing right in front of me. The whole office is probably listening, but I can't help myself. Archie has me rattled.

"It's not good enough, but it's a start. I want you to reverse the damage of me being called the anti-boyfriend." He turns and starts to leave my office.

It seems being known as a bad boyfriend has hit a nerve. When I first saw him, I'd judged him as a heartbreaker, and now other people are seeing him that way too. I shouldn't have been so quick to write him off. He's pushy, but his heart's in the right place. "I'll try," I say as he walks out of the door.

Archibald Banks doesn't like to be played for a fool,

and it's understandable to a degree. I can see his point, although I think he's over-reacting. It can't be nice to have your picture ripped up on social media, but it's not like all these women hate him. He's become an icon for women's beliefs. It's a protest of sorts. Once Christmas is over, everyone will forget, and hopefully, it won't seem so bad.

By the time I've managed to get him out of my office, I'm ready for a break. I message Morgan and get a couple of her pictures, which I upload to my social media accounts. Then Melanie messages Jake to upload one of the pictures to my designer page. I'm now aboard the Archibald Banks train, full steam ahead.

Instead of taking my coffee in the canteen, I step out onto the London streets. This morning, everything was going too well, but now I feel unsettled. One model's opinion shouldn't matter to me, yet he's got under my skin. Finding a quiet spot in the city is hard, so I head to the riverside, hoping the Thames will calm my mood.

My phone rings and my mother's face appears on the screen. I used to get excited for her calls, but since I left design school, I've accepted the truth. Our relationship will never be like it was when I was a child. She isn't supportive of my career the way I'd like her to be, and it's put a strain on our relationship. She's more interested in my social life, but my work takes up all my free time.

"Hello," I say when I answer. She should be heading to the Bahamas with my dad in a week, so she's probably called to check on me before she goes.

"Hello, darling. You kept him quiet." She sounds excited as she practically screams down the phone.

"Who?"

"Your new boyfriend, silly."

What is she talking about? "I…" She cuts me off before I get a chance to explain.

"Just in time for us to go to the winter ball at Ascot."

Oh. She must have seen my photos of me with Archie.

Now she has my attention. The event is used to celebrate the year's successes, and the guest list isn't something I'm usually added to. My mother has the power in the family and the money to match it. She owns a shipping company that imports goods from overseas. Her connections in the business world are deep. She hasn't attended the ball for years, and I'm never invited. "What happened to your holiday?"

"I'd like to spend some time with you. Is it serious with your new man?"

"Archibald?" I need clarity as she hasn't told me what she's seen.

"What a classic name. Is he from the London area?" Surely there's nobody else she could think I'm dating.

My mother is a bit of a snob. Having good pedigree and a respectable place in society is important to her.

It's part of the reason she wouldn't usually invite me to the Ascot Ball. Rebel Jacks doesn't exactly scream elite, and I'm not dating someone with connections. She'd be more impressed if one prince was wearing my designs than ten thousand regular people. However, I know very little about the guy I'm supposed to be seeing, so I guess I'm going to have to make it up.

"I think so," I say. Not my smoothest answer, but I need to figure Archie out. Any answer I give, I'll need to remember later.

"It's good to pay attention when a potential suitor is talking to you. Honestly. Haven't I taught you anything? I have to get back to my charity meeting, but I'll get my receptionist to email you the details. I'll see you on Saturday. Don't be late." She puts the phone down, yet again cutting off my response.

I'd love to go to the event, even if I have to work two days solid to make the perfect dress. If I turn up solo, my mother will let me stay but might not invite me to future events like this. She's always telling me love is what makes the world go around, but I want her to see it's my talent that makes me happy. I have a real opportunity to impress my mother and maybe get someone interested in my work. David Lorelson is royalty in the fashion industry, and he always attends the ball. If I could get him to notice me as more than the starry-eyed kid he probably remembers me as, I might be able to persuade him to showcase some of my designs in his annual fashion show. Before I can stop myself, I pull out my purse and find Archie's card. Once I've typed in the number, I hit dial, putting the phone up to my ear.

"Hello," he says after a few rings.

"Hi, Archie. It's Victoria. I've added your picture to my social media accounts, and I've reached out to my boss. Listen, I have an event on Saturday night that I'd like you to attend with me. It might be good for your dating image." I cringe, waiting for him to speak.

He takes a few seconds to answer me. "I'm sorry, I'm working. You'll have to find someone else."

I glance at the card. "No one else will do. It has to be you. How much notice do people usually give you to rent you as a date?"

"The business cards are old and were a joke from one of my friends."

I need a new angle if I'm going to convince him this is worth his time. "Okay, let's talk money. I'll give you five hundred pounds for one night." I doubt waiting tables offers that good a wage.

He takes a deep breath. "You like to get your own way, don't you?"

I ball my hand into a fist. He's making me sound like my mother. He's the one who's marched into my personal space on two occasions and made demands. But if I let my temper get the better of me, he'll probably hang up. "We'll have the opportunity to be photographed together, and it will be good exposure. If you do this, I'll also be in your debt."

"Why do you want me so badly?"

That's a loaded question. I put my attraction to him to one side. "Because my mother thinks we're dating, and that's the reason I got the invite." I can't think of a better reason than the truth that doesn't make me sound like a desperate singleton or interested in dating him for real.

"You want me to pretend to be your boyfriend?"

"Isn't that what the rent a date service is for?"

He's silent for a while. "Six hundred. You have to hire my suit and organise my transport. Also, I expect to be included in any of your social media posts."

His demands aren't much of a sacrifice. Instead of just a dress, I can make both outfits and claim the work for my portfolio. "Okay."

"And just one more thing."

"Name it."

"I want the opportunity to try out for your spring collection."

"Done." Yes. I've struck a deal. We say a brief goodbye before hanging up. I enjoy my coffee before walking back to my office. I smile at Melanie as I make my way inside. Kicking off my shoes, I sit at my desk, ready to work.

These daisies are going to need something extra special to get men interested in my shirts. When I think of flowers, I see perfume and women's clothing.

If I want to convince men to buy my design, I need it to have sex appeal. Spending the day looking at Archie's toned body won't be a problem, not that I'm expecting to get featured in Gallant again. At worst, he'll be one of the models on the Rebel Jacks website. At best, I'll be able to stare at his abs on my morning commute. This deal doesn't sound so bad.

What could possibly go wrong?

CHAPTER FIVE

I arrive at Archie's apartment with his suit over one arm. The navy-blue colour is going to look great on him. Once I knock, he lets me in, wearing only his boxers.

"You could've put some clothes on," I say trying to hold eye level. My mouth goes dry, and I moisten my lips with my tongue.

"What would be the point when I had to change when you arrived?" He takes the pale blue shirt first, and I watch him button it up. Next, the trousers zip into place before he puts on the jacket. I fuss over him until everything's in place. He hasn't changed since I originally took his measurements for the first audition. The suit fits perfectly. It's smart, and he's handsome in it.

"You look great."

"As do you." He gives a sharp nod of his head.

"Thanks. The fabric is from India and was woven together from the finest silk. This dress is a pretty big deal, and I designed both our outfits myself." I give him a twirl. We're matching. My dress is also a deep, rich blue with a sweetheart neckline and fishtail skirt. I didn't have as much time as I would've liked to make it, but I'm happy with the way it turned out. All the small imperfections are hidden from view.

"You're very talented."

A warm blush creeps over my skin. I'm proud of my work and I like his praise. If he softens me up, he might have me drooling over him more than I already am. "There are a few things you should know about tonight." He raises an eyebrow. I hand over the money. It's probably best to start with a positive. "Don't let my mother get you on her own. She'll grill you on your heritage. All the single women will only be interested in finding rich husbands. There will be some connections to the fashion industry, and I'll try to introduce you if I can. Oh, and you can keep the suit."

"What have you told your mother about us?" He smiles mischievously and I want to roll my eyes.

"She presumed we were dating when she saw the pictures of us together and I didn't correct her." I shrug like it's not a big deal, but it is. My mother wants me to be happy in a relationship, and I lied to her.

"Anything else?"

"No. I think we're all set." I smile tightly and he nods.

I'm a little nervous. Archie can handle himself, but I've never pretended to date someone before.

He puts on his blue patent leather shoes. I leave the garment bag hanging over a chair and grab my clutch bag. He puts his wallet into his pocket before grabbing his keys. He leads me out of the door and then locks it behind us.

We walk down to the car and sit in the back of the limousine that I hired from a friend of the family. I often use the company for important events. Archie looks impressed as he gets comfy in his seat. During the drive, I check my emails and look at the feedback from my boss about the spring collection. I can feel Archie's eyes on me as I read. My pulse quickens, and subtly, I look up at him. He smiles as I try not to blush. It's been a long time since I had the company of a man and I feel awkward.

Once we arrive, we enter the luxurious ballroom. The black and white room has been glamourised with lavish gold décor. There's a balloon arch over the stage area, martini glass pyramids next to a chocolate fountain, and glitter everywhere. I've been in this room a few times before, and even plain, it's glorious. The black and white marble floor is striking. "That's a beautiful dress, Victoria," one of my mother's friends, Regena, says.

"Thank you. I designed and made it myself."

"You have been busy." She eyes up my date. "And who is this handsome man?"

"Regena Olsen, meet Archibald Banks. Regena owns

a private yacht company. Archibald is an up-and-coming model." I gesture to him proudly.

"Hello, Archibald. You look magnificent," Regena says, a little too enthusiastically.

"It's a pleasure to meet you. Victoria designed my suit too." Archie instantly steps into a flirty persona.

"And you look divine in it." She's looking at him as if he's a yummy snack. It's cringeworthy considering she's old enough to be his mother, but I just smile politely.

"You're too kind. The dress you're wearing is exquisite. I'm lucky enough to have two lovely ladies in front of me." He smiles kindly. It's like he has a switch where he can turn on the charm whenever he's trying to impress someone. It works too. Regena is like putty in his hands.

"Victoria, you are a lucky woman. Archibald is a delight." She touches his arm like they're already good friends.

"Thanks."

"There you are," my mother says as she comes over to us. She embraces me, and I try not to tense.

"Where has she been hiding her boyfriend, Edith?" Regena says to my mother.

"Nowhere he can't be found." They both laugh.

My mother's been trying to match me up for a while, and she seems happy I've finally found a relationship.

Personally, I thought she would disapprove of Archie until she knew he was more than a pretty face, but clearly, I was wrong.

"Is he joining us at the lodge for Christmas?" Regena asks as if neither of us are standing right next to her.

"Maybe," my mother says without consulting me. I'm confused about what lodges she's talking about. My mum usually stays in a five-star hotel during the festive period. She doesn't go with Regena, and I'm never invited.

"Wait. I thought your trip to the Bahamas was postponed?" I ask, trying to catch up. There's something she hasn't told me.

"Yes, it was. Your father and I are going for the New Year. We're spending Christmas here in England. Let's go get a drink." She tugs on Archie's arm as she makes it clear I'm not invited to join. I'm about to object when I spot David Lorelson and his wife. He hosts a fashion show every year, and I'd love to be part of the line-up. Abandoning the thought of saving my date, I move over to them.

"Victoria Ainsworth, is that really you?" Lucy Lorelson asks.

"Hello, Mr and Mrs Lorelson." I curtsy, wishing I had that magic switch Archie uses to turn on the charm. "How is your daughter?" I haven't seen Isabella in years, but she always seemed keen to follow in her father's footsteps.

"Please call us David and Lucy. We're all friends here.

Isabella's seventeen now and debuting her first teen collection tonight. How is your job in London going?"

"That's great. I love designing clothes and seeing new collections. Rebel Jacks is treating me well, thank you." I don't seem to have David's full attention, as he's looking around the room for something, but I'm not ready to give up yet.

"I'm pleased you're enjoying the city. I'm sure we'll catch up later. Excuse us," David says, proving I was right. I never mentioned the city.

"I designed my dress and my date's suit," I add as they leave. For a second, I close my eyes. That did not go smoothly. When I'm composed, I try again with a few other couples. Unfortunately, by the time I'm sitting down for the main event, I'm all struck out.

Archie escorts my mother to her seat before sitting next to me. "What have you been talking about all this time?" I ask him, hoping he hasn't blown our cover. I didn't want him to cosy up with her. It wasn't my choice for them to go to the bar together. If she finds out I hired him so I could get a ticket, she won't be impressed.

"Edith's been telling me stories from her modelling days." They share a smile.

Unease settles in my stomach. I don't want to get caught out. He's using my mum's first name and he's letting her reminisce about the one time she stepped in for a fashion show. If she asks even the smallest detail about me or my so-called relationship, she might figure out it's fake. I bite my tongue. I'm ready to write this whole evening off as a disaster and go back to my sketch book. "After the meal, let me introduce you to some designers?" I want to get him away from my mother and I'm hoping he'll like this idea.

"This evening's about meeting the wonderful woman who brought you into the world."

My mother actually blushes, and I try not to gasp. *That is not what this evening is about.* "You, Archibald Banks, are a real treat."

"Thank you."

I frown. He met my mother less than an hour ago and they seem like best friends. She's never liked any of my previous boyfriends and she usually pushes me towards the business types.

"Excuse me. I need to powder my nose." I excuse myself and head to the nearest bathroom. I'm not sure why I'm so upset. I like Archie. I just wish my mother was this supportive of my career rather than my relationship status.

I push the swing door and walk inside the ladies' room.

"I can't wear this dress. Everyone will laugh," I hear a young woman say.

"If you hadn't been drinking red wine, this wouldn't have happened," a familiar voice replies.

"I only had a sip. It was Tina's fault for not watching where she was going and knocking into me."

I walk towards the voices and the cubicle area.

"You're not eighteen for another couple of months."

Lucy and Isabella stop talking when they see me. Her dress looks like something was murdered on it. The once pretty pink dress is ruined, and no amount of dabbing with paper towels is going to change that.

"I'm sorry. I didn't mean to interrupt." I go into one of the cubicles to use the toilet. I'm about to fasten myself back into my dress as a sob leaves Isabella's lips.

I may not always make the right decision when I go after what I want, but I have a heart. Instead of tidying myself up, I remove my dress, putting it over one arm. Unlocking the door, I step back into the main room of the bathroom in my matching Victoria's Secret underwear. They both stare at me like I've lost my mind. I guess it's not every day you see a half-naked woman. "I think we're about the same size." I'm body proud so I don't try to cover myself over. I was taught confidence is beauty in fashion school.

"Who is the designer?" Isabella asks. Her gaze is on my dress, and my lack of clothing seems to be acceptable under the circumstances.

I wanted to have my name on the Lorelson lips, but this isn't quite how I pictured it. You'd think she'd be happy with any clean dress while in a crisis, but apparently not.

"It's a Victoria Ainsworth original. I made it myself."

My answer must satisfy her as she holds her hands out for it. Ten minutes later, we've switched outfit, and I'm leaving the bathroom in a stained dress.

My mother gasps when I return to the table. Her hands fly to her mouth as she stares at me in horror. "What happened?"

"You'll have to wait and see," I say cryptically.

The waiter serves tomato soup. Archie tucks his napkin into the neckline of his shirt, and I look at the mess on my dress. It probably wouldn't matter if I spilt anything, but I decide to copy him. The dress is not mine.

"This suit is too nice to risk spilling soup on it," Archie says.

A warm feeling settles over me. I'm glad he likes my craftsmanship enough to protect it. "Will you wear it again?" I ask.

"Definitely." He sounds so sure I can't help but smile. He dips his spoon into his bowl and starts eating. "This is delicious."

I pick up my spoon and taste the soup. "Yes. It's good."

We all start to eat. "Which designers are here that you want to talk to?" Archie asks.

"There are a few people here." I don't name drop because we're with my mum.

"Tell me, Archie, where do your parents live?" mum asks.

"I'm local to London. My parents live near Hyde Park."

"What do they do for work?"

I hold my breath because I'm not sure what the answer is, and I don't want my mum to turn her nose up at him. "My dad works as a mechanic for BMW, and my mum is a receptionist in the office."

"Oh," Mum says before smiling sympathetically. She wasn't expecting him to say that, and she takes a few seconds to compose herself.

"I drive a BMW," Regena says.

"I wish I had one," Archie says, making them both laugh.

"I haven't passed my driving test," I say, trying to join in the conversation and soften the blow to my mother's dreams of me dating a rich man.

"Why is that?" Archie asks.

"Yes. Why is that?" my mum echoes. All attention turns to me.

I shrug. "Nobody drives in London."

"Someone drove us here," Archie says.

The soup bowls are collected when we're finished.

"I couldn't park a car near my apartment, and we got here fine. There's no reason for me to drive."

"Have I discovered something Victoria Ainsworth isn't good at?" Archie asks, covering his mouth like he's shocked.

"Don't get used to it, Archibald. Victoria likes to be the best," Mum says.

"I know she does," Archie replies and winks at me.

I want to argue, but I *am* competitive.

For the next course, a roast dinner is served. A string quartet begins to play, and we eat in silence while listening to the music.

"That was beautiful," I say when the piece of music finishes.

"When I was a kid, I used to play the violin," Archie says.

"Me too." I smile. I can't imagine him playing such a small instrument. A guitar or the drums seems more likely.

"You'll have to perform a duet for us one day," Mum says.

"I'm rusty," Archie answers.

"I'm not sure about that." I shake my head.

We have ice cream for dessert, which is as good as the other two courses.

David Lorelson taps on his glass while standing on the stage next to the large staircase. He talks about his achievements over the last year before introducing his daughter. Isabella appears in my dress, looking radiant. Everyone claps, and her smile makes swapping dresses worth it. She introduces her collection, which appears on a big screen behind her, and begins to talk about the individual pieces. She's great at public speaking.

"Now your dress change makes sense," Archie says.

"When I saw her in the bathroom, I knew I had to help." I'm pleased I could help and love seeing my design on stage, even if the teen wear is the centrepiece.

"It was very kind of you to swap outfits," Mum says.

"Well done, Victoria, for saving the day," Regena says.

"Thanks, everyone."

After the food and speeches, I introduce Archie to a few designers, including David Lorelson.

"Mr Lorelson I'd like you to meet Archibald Banks. Mr Lorelson sponsors fashion events and has a catwalk event once a year. Archibald is a model and was featured in this season's Gallant."

They shake hands. "It's nice to meet you," Archie

says.

"Isabella showed me your advert. I think she has a crush," David says, smiling kindly.

"It was an honour to be featured." Archie stands taller with a satisfied grin on his face.

I smile and put my arm on Archie. "I'm not surprised she has a crush. He looks great."

"And in your design too. Well done both of you." David tilts his glass towards us.

"Thanks," we both say in unison. I'm grateful Isabella showed our ad to her father, and it's great to hear him acknowledge it.

Over the next hour, we work our way around the room, making small talk. A few more designers show their work on the stage, and I enjoy having Archie's company.

When Archie goes to the bar to get us a drink, my mother comes to stand with me. "I'm glad you came tonight," she says.

"Thank you for inviting me."

"It's good to see you happy with a man." She gestures over to where Archie is standing. He's talking to the bartender.

My smile wavers. My relationship status is at the forefront of her mind, as usual. I shouldn't be surprised. "Archie's a good guy." I glance at him again. I'm glad it's him who's here with me. He's been good company and makes the little digs from my mother bearable.

"Yes. He seems nice." She smiles.

I'm waiting for a but… it never comes. "We're going to have one more drink and then head out."

"I'm waiting for your father to pick me up and then I'm going. I'll call you later in the week." Her phone chimes and she reads the message. "He's outside now."

My gut twists. I miss my dad a lot, but his absence tonight rings loudly. He's not ready to forgive me for going against his wishes by not marrying Alexander.

"Okay." I nod. She gives me a hug before we say our goodnights.

Archie returns with two glasses of wine. "I just saw your mum. She said she was leaving."

"Yes. She came to say goodbye."

He passes me one of the glasses. "I don't know why you were so weird about me spending time with her. She's great." He takes a sip of his wine.

"My mum sometimes has a one-track mind. She wants me to get married more than anything." I take a gulp of my drink. The sweet taste is zesty on my tongue.

"Is it so bad she wants you to find someone?"

I shrug. "I'd like it more if she was gushing over my

dress. I don't need a boyfriend."

"Maybe you should tell her how you feel."

"Maybe." I'm not sure I want to have that conversation with her. Isn't a parent supposed to know what will make their child happy?

Archie and I make small talk while we finish our wine.

"Congratulations," I say to Isabella on our way out and pass her a card with my address on it so she can return my dress.

"Thank you. You saved my night."

"It was the right thing to do. I can see you worked hard to get prepared for your presentation."

We smile at each other. "Thank you."

"What would you like me to do with your dress? I can take it to the laundrette and see if they can salvage it?" I look down at the stain. It would take a miracle to get the wine out of the fabric.

She shakes her head with a frown. "No, it's fine. You can throw it. I won't wear it again anyway."

"Okay. Enjoy the rest of the party. Goodnight." I give a sympathetic smile because we both know the truth. There's no saving it.

She gives me a loose hug, careful not to press our dresses together. "Goodnight."

Once outside, I call for my ride home.

"You did a good deed tonight," Archie says once we're alone.

"I have a way of being won over by people in need." I smile coyly.

"I had fun." He sounds surprised by his statement. *Was he expecting it to be boring?*

"Me too. I hope something good comes out of it for you." I clasp my hands together, hoping to show empathy. If Archie gets a casting call out of this, I'll be happy.

"It already has." He smiles, gazing into my eyes. I'm not sure I understand the meaning of his words, but I can't help being mesmerised by him.

We eye each other for a few seconds.

It's been a strange evening. I got what I wanted in a round-about way, and I enjoyed spending time with my mum. It's been a long time since I felt relaxed in her company, even with her talking about my relationship more than my work. She and Archie surprised me too. Despite their differences, they seemed to like each other.

The journey is mostly silent as tiredness washes over me. When we arrive at Archie's home, he leans in to kiss me on the cheek, and I turn my head too quickly, accidentally headbutting him.

"Oh, gosh. I'm so sorry." Pain throbs through my skull.

Archie rubs his head. "No, it's my fault for surprising you. I just wanted to say goodnight."

"Goodnight," I say lamely.

That could've gone smoother.

He gets out of the car, and I hold my forehead before I can make the situation worse. We leave things on good terms, but I'm certain we have unfinished business.

CHAPTER SIX

It's two weeks until Christmas, and Rebel Jacks is shutting down for the holidays. I'm taking some of my work home so I can continue on my designs.

"Don't you ever want to take a break?" Melanie asks.

"What for?"

"Since your mother's going to the Winter Lodges in Cornwall, why don't you be the Ainsworth abroad this Christmas?" She holds her hands up like she's unmasking a genius plan.

"No. I'd rather stay in England."

"Since your mum's chosen to stay in the country, have you considered joining your family in the south?"

"I'm not sure why my mother has chosen to stay in the cold, but I realised the second she said I had to bring Archie I couldn't go." I don't mention that my brother is probably somewhere in Europe.

"Have you spoken to either of them since the ball?" She looks concerned, but there's no need.

"No. I haven't had a reason to talk to Archie, and I've spoken to my mother, but all she wants to know is the lowdown on my boyfriend and how our relationship is going. It's too much." Archie is a nice guy, but I'm not looking for a man or even a new friend. Other than trying to kiss my cheek, he hasn't made any advances. He gave no sign he's interested in dating me. Besides, my work consumes me, and I like it that way. Even if I could have something with him, my busy schedule would probably get in the way. I can't commit to any kind of relationship. He could get bored of me, and I hate break-ups.

I shake off the thought. Why am I imagining our whole relationship? I've smoothed over the cardigan incident. Instead of being hung up on what could be, I'm going to enjoy my Christmas with my sketchpad and lounge pants while forgetting everyone else exists.

"You didn't ask for my opinion, but we're friends, so I'm going to give you it anyway. Honestly, I think you like the guy and you're scared to take a chance on him." She puts her hands on her hips, giving me some of her usual sass.

"I don't know how I feel about Archie. The Ascot Ball didn't go to plan, although it was nice to have him there."

It's not that I don't know what my feelings for Archie

are. It's more I don't know what to do with them. Melanie understands how badly I'd like to be seen in the fashion world. I want to be one of the best. I would've liked to have left the event with a contact for something new. A place on the catwalk or a commission for an outfit. That was the goal at the ball.

"Isabella Lorelson wore your dress and hasn't returned it yet. I'd say that's a small success."

"I guess." My lips turn up into a faint smile.

"Come here and give me a hug." We move closer and she squeezes me unnecessarily tight.

We break apart, and I feel a lot better. Getting the details of the Ascot Ball off my chest is what I needed. Melanie is a good friend, my shoulder to cry on, and my advisor. Even if I don't always follow her advice, I want to hear it. I've tried to avoid talking about Archie, yet she still knew he was on my mind.

"Has my work been completely packed up?" I pick up my sketches from this morning and file them in my portfolio.

"Yes, it has. It's only you that's lingering around the office. Your boxes are downstairs, waiting for you to call your driver." Melanie puts my pencils away.

"Is everything else finished up? Do you have your work phone charged?" I move the fabric samples into the boxes at the side of my desk. I won't be taking them home, but I'd like to come back to a tidy workspace.

"I'm leaving the business mobile in the drawer where it belongs. Your only emergency contact this holiday will be the Lucky City Chinese takeout. I'm taking two weeks with my family as I promised them. I'll be sipping mulled wine and sitting with my feet up. I'm ready to leave as soon as you give me the word." I glance at my watch. It's not even lunchtime yet. She stands tall, staring at me.

It's Christmas. I shouldn't be taking her away from her family. "Okay. You're right. I'll try and relax. You leave your work in the office and I'll do what I always do. *The opposite.* Let's go say goodbye to Jake, then get out of here before I change my mind." I put my arm around her shoulder, and we start to leave my office.

"Now that sounds like a plan." She squeezes me again.

We make our rounds of the building, which is almost empty, before my driver picks me up. "Goodbye," I say to Melanie.

"Merry Christmas," she says with a wave. I leave my assistant at the side of Rebel Jacks, ready to spend two weeks all alone.

The cold breeze makes me pull my coat up as I step out of the car. I make my way upstairs to my apartment. The driver, George, will bring my things up, and I leave him to it. To my surprise, on my doorstep is a bouquet of white roses with thistles. There's a large box propped up on the frame of the door. I smile as excitement bubbles in my stomach.

Who would send me flowers for Christmas?

I unlock my apartment door and carry everything inside. George passes me my work, and when I'm unpacked, I kick off my shoes. The dress I lent to Isabella is in the box with a card. It reads:

Thank you for saving the day. The dress is beautifully made, and it was an honour to borrow it. See you at the Winter Lodges. From the Lorelson Family.

I'd hurried the sewing and gone for a simpler design than I would have liked. All the errors and cover-up techniques come rushing back to me. Hopefully, there wasn't anything too noticeable.

My attention turns to the beautiful flowers. I put them in a vase from under the sink, filled with water, before putting them in the centre of my small dining table.

Over the next hour, I get comfortable with my sketchbook until there's a knock at the door. When I open it, I'm greeted by my mother. I try to cover my surprise but fail. She hardly ever comes down here and I'm suspicious.

"Hello, darling," she says.

"Hello. What are you doing here?" I fight hard to cover my shock. I should be happy to see her, but I'm nervous. My apartment is a mess. I would've tidied up if I'd known she was coming. I expect her to call from her holiday destination, not to visit last-minute and throw me off balance.

"I've come to check on you since you're not answering my calls." She hugs me. It's true, I've been avoiding her, but only because I don't want to talk about my fake boyfriend. She wanted me to marry straight out of school, and I wanted to go to the London School of Design. Even though we talk at least once a month, relationships have always been a touchy subject between us.

"I've been busy with work and forgot to call you back. When you phoned, I was sketching and then thinking about cooking risotto for lunch. I hadn't paid much attention to my mobile." My excuses are lame, but I don't know what else to say.

She looks around my apartment, taking it in. My work is everywhere and there's no room for me to have company. My mum couldn't sit on the sofa unless she made space. She hasn't tried to make herself comfortable as she stands awkwardly in between my drawings and shirt prototypes. "If I'd known Archibald had broken your heart, I'd have been more sensitive."

"What? Archie didn't break anything." I'm offended she's jumped to this conclusion. Just because I haven't tidied up doesn't mean I'm going through a bad time. If I had a boyfriend, maybe he'd be okay with the mess. I've been working, but my apartment is clean, just cluttered. Besides who's to say the reason Archie isn't here has anything to do with us breaking up? For all she knows, he could be at work, out with friends, or even taking a nap.

"Then where is he? Surely he wouldn't leave you

alone at Christmas." She continues to scrutinise my living space. You'd think I'd left dirty plates all over with the way she's turning her nose up.

"It's Friday, not Christmas Eve. He's probably at work." I shrug.

Should I tell her the whole thing was a charade to get an invite to the ball? I've gotten away with avoiding the truth and no harm has come of it. I should keep my mouth shut.

"Is that why you're not coming to The Winter Lodges? Everyone is expecting you, and from what I've heard, David Lorelson wants to talk to you."

My mother hasn't been interested in my work before, so I mistrust her motives. "Why did you invite me to the ball?" I ask, trying not to raise a suspicious eyebrow.

"I wanted to spend time with you and your boyfriend." She smiles.

"Why are you telling me about Mr Lorelson, then?" I frown. I usually avoid asking her direct questions like this.

"What do you mean?" Her frown matches mine.

"You've never tried to set me up with a fashion contact before."

"I don't know why he wants to talk to you." She shrugs. Maybe she didn't think it was business-related, or she's willing to do anything to get me to come to the Winter Lodges. At a guess, there's something she's not telling me.

"I've decided to have a quiet Christmas at home." I fake a huge smile like this is going to be the best Christmas ever.

"That's what you do every year. Go pack a bag and I'll call Archibald so I can convince him this Christmas should be spent with the whole Ainsworth family." She points towards my bedroom like it's an order.

"How are you going to call Archie? You don't have his number, do you?" They didn't spend that much time together. Surely, he didn't give her his contact details.

"No, but I could get it from you. I'm sure he wouldn't mind." She seems confident he would be okay with her calling.

"No. Archie can't make it."

"Don't be silly. Once I explain, he'll have to come." Her tone tells me she's determined to get her way.

"Why is it important we come?" We stare at each other for a few seconds before she looks away.

"We haven't spent much time together as a family, and your brother will be there too." There's a desperation to her tone. Her pitch is higher than usual, and she's talking as if there's an urgency to get me to agree to come.

Charles hasn't been in England for more than a weekend in years. Something doesn't seem right, and she's only giving me minimal information.

"I'll pack a bag, but I don't think Archie will be able to join us." A week with my family won't be so bad if it makes my mum happy. I can tell she'll be disappointed if I refuse to go. Besides, I can take my work with me and maybe talk about how important it is to me so she understands why it's my main priority. When I left for design school, we didn't talk about that, and we left things between us in a difficult place.

"Just go get ready." She pokes her finger back towards my bedroom door. I could tell her I'd catch up with her tomorrow, but I don't want to give myself chance to get cold feet. I've avoided her, so instead of her convincing me to go to the Winter Lodges with plenty of time to pack I won't have long to get my things.

I nod and disappear into my bedroom. Since starting at Rebel Jacks, I haven't taken much annual leave, and although I could be working from home, it will be nice to have some quality time with my family. Hopefully, I'll get a chance to work things out with my parents, and I'd like to see my brother. I like listening to Charles's stories, and I haven't spoken to my dad in a while. Since I went to design school, things between us have been strained. This could be an opportunity to try and make my relationships better with my whole family.

I grab my suitcase and fill it with winter clothes. Once I have all the essentials, I look for my portfolio in case I get a chance to pitch ideas to David Lorelson. Regena mentioned a few families would be at the lodges, and I'm guessing they've made a group booking for exclusivity. I finish filling my bag by throwing in a few pencils.

My mother's on the phone when I reappear looking for my sketchbook.

"So, you'll come?" my mother says to the person she's engrossed in conversation with.

She pauses to listen to their reply. Then she says, "Victoria, he wants to speak to you."

My pulse quickens when I notice she's been using my mobile. She holds it out to me, and Archie's name is on the screen.

I hold my breath and count to three before taking the phone. I plaster on a fake smile, even though he can't see it. "Hi, Archie," I say with way too much enthusiasm.

"Can your mother hear us?" he asks in a low voice.

"I don't think so, but give me a second." I move toward the kitchen area. "Go ahead," I say, hoping there's enough distance between my mother and me.

"Five thousand for just over a week and I'll throw in a Christmas present. I promise to be the perfect date and I'll be attentive to all your needs." He's all business with me, but I guess that's how I've treated him from the start of our strange relationship.

I want to ask him why he's willing to leave his family at Christmas, but I'll have to wait until we're in private before we can talk freely. *Am I really considering this?* If I take him with me, I'll have an excuse to go to my room or take a walk. I love my mother, but spending twenty-four-seven with her for over a week might be too much. Five thousand isn't a lot of money for someone like me. I come from old money and have a large trust fund. My great-great-grandfather used to build cargo ships, so it's not like I'm short on cash. My mother used his connections to set up her own company in the shipping industry, and the Ainsworth name is something I'm proud of. We're all ambitious in our own way, even if we don't always get it right. "I thought you had to work?"

"This *is* work. I can pick up a new waiting or bar job any time. I also saw Mr Lorelson at a casting call and he wants to talk about the fashion show. I'm going to meet with him in the new year, and I'm hoping he'll give me a job. You seemed interested in working with him at the ball. Maybe he'll consider your designs. Maybe we can talk to him together. I can meet you at Paddington Station in an hour."

I could argue or ask for more information about what he'll do once we get to the lodges, but to be honest, I think I'm getting a good deal. He was great at the ball and made it easier for me to talk to people. Renting a date couldn't be easier. "Okay. I'll see you then."

"Excellent."

I hang up the phone and my Christmas for one has just become a festival for a village.

With a little persuasion, my mother leaves me to meet Archie at the station with two tickets to Truro, Cornwall. I could've got a driver to pick him up, but as he suggested meeting at Paddington station, I might as well use the journey to get our story straight without anyone overhearing us. Plus, as Melanie says, it's the time of year to give my staff a break. Christmas holiday, here I come.

CHAPTER SEVEN

The station's busy when I arrive, and there are so many people moving around, I can't see Archie. I drag my bag towards the timetables board. Our train is on schedule, which is a relief. I hate when my travel gets delayed. My skin prickles, and as I look over my shoulder, I see him. Archie looks his cool, gorgeous self as he approaches me under the board. "Hi," I say.

"Hello. We need to be on platform seven B." He checks his watch.

I open the front pocket of my suitcase. "Here's your ticket, and I've transferred the money into your bank account." I pulled up the details from the company database.

"Thank you." He puts the ticket in his coat pocket, then he leans in and kisses my cheek.

"What was that for?" I step back to make sure he doesn't do it again.

"If we're going to pull this off, there can't be any weirdness between us. That kiss was my apology."

He could regret any number of his actions, but I'm guessing he's talking about the outburst in my office. "I'm sorry too. I should've been more considerate of your feelings when I chose to change the winter campaign." It feels good to get that off my chest. I want us to be friends while we're away.

"Unless you want your family to figure out we're not dating, you can't pull away from me if I show you affection." Amusement dances across his face.

"I'm not the sort of person who would be intimate in public." He's probably trying to get a rise out of me, and it's working. I'm completely out of the dating game and it's going to be strange having Archie in my space. After an awkward pause, we start walking through the station.

"Maybe not, but if you don't show subtle kindness, someone will guess." He shrugs.

"We can be friends," I say lamely. I need to relax or it will be obvious we're not a couple. I hadn't thought this through, and my palms begin to feel sweaty.

We reach the platform, and the train doesn't take long to arrive. The door opens, and we get on. Our reserved seats are in first class, and Archie puts our luggage into the designated area.

"If you don't want to sell us as a couple, why bring me at all?" He bites his bottom lip like he's thinking too hard.

The whistle goes off to signal the train is about to move. I stare out the window as we set off. I brought him so it would be easier for me to get through this holiday. If I want Archie on my side, I'm going to have to be honest with him. My half-truths and betrayal have probably shaken his trust in me. I need him to understand my reasoning so he doesn't abandon the plan at the first sign of trouble.

"My mother invited you. When I realised she was on the phone with you, it was easier to agree to your terms than admit I'm a liar who has deceived her. Having you at the Winter Lodges should help everything run smoothly as my mum desperately wants me to settle down. You being there will get her off my back. You're a charismatic guy and I'm glad you decided to come."

He smooths down his hair, taking a second to think about his words. "I can see you like to be in control of situations."

"You say that like it's a bad thing, but honestly, I'm not one for surprises. Plus, if I hadn't taken charge of my destiny, I'd be married to Alexander Huntington the third instead of following my dreams in fashion." His name reels off my tongue like I'm bored of mentioning him. I went to school with Alexander and although we never dated, I always liked him. He's not the problem. It was the way he was rammed down my throat. *Alexander has this. Alexander can offer you that.*

"Alexander Huntington the third sounds like a drag. I'm joking, but I understand you a little more now." He smiles.

"Alexander is a nice guy. That wasn't the problem. But he has to travel a lot for work, and he wanted a family right away. I wasn't ready for it."

"And what about now?" He tips his head to the side.

"I've learned so much working for Rebel Jacks, and I'm grateful for the opportunities they've given me." I clasp my hands together on the table.

He frowns. "This isn't a job interview. What do you really want?"

"I'd like my own clothing brand. Both casual and formal attire."

"And what about a relationship?"

I twist my hair over one shoulder. "It's been a while since I dated. It's hard to find someone who fits into my busy work schedule. Anyway, enough about me. What about you? Do you have a girlfriend?" It's unlikely he does but I want him to spell it out. The idea of him seeing someone else fills me with unease. I've never wanted someone to tell me they're single as much as I need him to. My dry spell means I'm practically a reborn virgin. It's been so long since I had any action that his kiss counts as foreplay.

"Nope. I'm like you. I work too much, and I don't like to depend on others." He clasps his hands and puts them on the table, mirroring my pose.

"Have you always wanted to be a model?"

"No. When my high school girlfriend broke up with

me, she said I should get a job posing in a shop window because I was only nice to look at."

"Ouch." This girl must've been a piece of work.

"It was my own fault. I wanted to go out with the hottest girl in school, but I spent all my time playing football. When I injured my knee, I realised we weren't compatible because I still didn't want to see her. I guess that makes me an asshole."

"I'm sorry things didn't work out."

He laughs. "Did you listen to what I said?"

"Yes. You're a pretty boy and you thought you needed a beautiful girl to make you look like you had your shit together."

He belly laughs. "I guess you're right. Back then, I thought football was going to change my life."

"And what about now?"

"Now I'm just getting by. I like modelling, and I have no problem waiting tables."

"Good for you. I have to ask, though… why were you so upset when Rose started advertising my cardigan?"

"Rose is my ex-girlfriend."

I cringe. Not only did I help crush his campaign, but I unknowingly helped Rose get revenge. My stomach knots. "I had no idea. I'm sorry."

"Don't worry about it. I did want to feature in the magazine, and I do want to model more of your clothes. You are a fantastic designer and I already own some of your t-shirts. That's why I tried to convince you that you were making a mistake by not choosing me."

"I'm flattered. It's also nice that you can adjust your dream."

"Yes. That's what happens when a football injury crushes your hopes and dreams. You have to make it work."

I feel bad he lost his chance at football, but I like his optimism. "What's your long-term goal?"

"To marry a rich fashion designer and be a stay-at-home dad." He winks at me to show he's joking.

"Very funny. If that was true, you would've flirted with me at the ball." I playfully pout, although it disappears quickly. *Am I the one flirting now?*

"I apologise for that. I was joking about my goals. The truth is, I don't have it all figured out, and it doesn't matter." He waves his hands like he's letting all his worries fade away.

Wait. Is he flirting back or being friendly? I decide to overlook whatever this may be. "Good for you."

"What are you hoping to get out of this trip?"

One of the guys from the drinks booth comes over with a trolley and we both order a cup of tea.

I think over his question for a moment. I'm not sure what the realistic answer is. I want my dad to forgive me for not following his and mum's plan. I want to have a good Christmas listening to the adventures I've missed. My heart is overwhelmed by all the things I wish I could have. I keep my answer as straightforward as I can. "It's been a long time since my family was all together. My mother wanted me to come, so here we are."

He nods. "How did we meet?"

"Let's keep it simple. You're a model and tried out for my winter collection. You got the job and I asked you on a date."

"Oh, I don't think so. I asked you on a date." He gives me a serious look.

I smile. "What, a woman can't go after the man she wants?"

"She absolutely can. But not you." He shakes his head, and he still has a stern look. I don't think he's going to back down on this.

I fold my arms. "Why not?"

"You're a control freak. I won't let you boss me around."

I fake a laugh. *I'm not that bad, am I?* I like to get my way, but I can give a little. "Do I intimidate you?"

"Absolutely not, but for you to fall for someone, I think you'd have to give up some of the control." He reaches over the table and strokes the back of my hand. Butterflies erupt in my stomach. He's only trying to prove a point and I need to remember that.

"A little affection over the Christmas period might be okay, and I can tell our story like you were the one instigating the relationship."

He smiles. "I knew you'd come around to my way of thinking."

My heart warms. It feels really good to have him close. I'm trying to work out what this change in me means, so I try to ignore the way he's making me feel. "What's your living quarters like?"

"I live in a shared house with a group of guys."

"That could get loud and messy." Archie strikes me as the sort of person that's sociable but also likes his own space.

"It can be. Living in London can be expensive, and it's better than the alternative. I can always escape to Hyde Park or visit my parents. It beats living under their roof." He scratches the back of his neck.

"Are you close with your family?"

"Yeah. I have two brothers who I'm tight with, and my parents are awesome." He smiles bigger than usual.

"Then why do you prefer living with the guys?" It seems like there's more to this story.

He chuckles. "Let's say some distance can make the

heart grow fonder."

I laugh. "I get that. I couldn't go back home now either." Even if I mend my relationship with my parents, I couldn't move home. The distance is needed to keep me sane.

We drink our tea and use the train ride to get to know each other. Archie is beautiful inside and out. Talking to him only makes my crush grow stronger. Bringing him will either be the best thing I've ever done or the worst.

CHAPTER EIGHT

When we arrive in Truro, we have a bit of time to kill. Even though it's late, we get food from a vending machine and sit on the benches in the train station. I open a pasty which, in these parts, shouldn't be bought in a prepacked wrapper.

"This is not a sight I ever thought I'd see," Archie says, twisting the lid off his bottle of Coke.

I brush my hair off my face. "I know I'm a mess."

"That's not what I meant. You always look beautiful. I meant slumming it with a cheap pasty and waiting for a ride."

My face heats at the compliment, even though he's probably just being polite. "I'm not that bad. I like nice clothes, but I don't have to have the best of everything. I'm not a food snob, plus, I can be patient when I need to be."

"Sure you can." He winks at me.

I nudge him with my elbow. "While we're away, you're going to get an eye-opener if that's what you think."

He holds his arms out wide. "Let's see it."

We eat our food while chatting. After an hour or so, my brother texts to say he's waiting for us. We gather up our things and exit the station. My brother's hard to miss. His light brown hair is combed back and he's wearing his Gucci jumper with jeans. "Hello, Charles," I say.

"Nice to see you, Victoria and… Archibald." He eyes him up. It's strange seeing my brother's mouth watering over one of my dates. He usually pretends to be bored.

I move up to my brother and pretend to push his jaw shut. "He's straight."

"Shame. I'm the fun Ainsworth." He winks at Archie.

I roll my eyes. "Archie is a trendsetter, not a fashion follower, unlike you with your overpriced jeans and last season's jumper. He's the kind of guy who turns heads."

"Yeah, I saw the anti-boyfriend thing. I'm sorry about that." He clenches his teeth. Me and my brother love to tease each other. It's our way of showing we care. If he's seen my Gallant campaign, that means he's been checking up on me, which makes me happy. If he's already pointing out Archie's flaws, he must be impressed with my boyfriend.

"I got the woman. The rest is fake news. It's great to finally meet you, Charles." Archie places his hands on my shoulders. He's already stepped into the role I need him to play and he's defusing the petty insults Charles and I are throwing at each other.

We get into the car and Charles drives us through the tiny country roads.

"How did Mum convince you to come on this trip? It's been about six years since we spent Christmas together," I ask my brother as I stare out the window. The tall bushes and high walls aren't much to look at, but I'm sure our destination will be beautiful.

"Reminding me how much time has passed was a factor. She also said she was postponing her trip abroad and wanted all of her family here."

I frown. "Do you think something could be wrong?"

"I didn't. Now I do, though." He glances at me through the central mirror and then looks back at the road. Archie rubs my forearm comfortingly. It's strange having someone other than my assistant trying to put me at ease.

We arrive at the Winter Lodges and unload the luggage. There's nothing but beautiful country views for miles, and the large holiday homes fit perfectly with their Christmas décor. There's fake snow on the roofs, light-up icicles, and giant baubles.

"Which one is ours?" I ask, meaning mine and

Archie's.

"We're sharing the large Dasher one." Charles points at a lodge that looks like it could sleep eight people. It's a lot of space for the three of us.

"How many people are coming? I thought we'd be in one of the smaller ones at the back."

Charles softly laughs. "If you thought you were getting a quiet getaway with your boyfriend, you're sadly mistaken. The whole family is staying here." He pulls my suitcase inside, and I wearily follow him.

My mum greets me like she hasn't already seen me today, and my aunt is here too. "I'm so glad you could make it," Mum says. I hug my family members, including my dad, who stands from the armchair in front of the TV. I hold onto him a little longer than the others. It's good to see him. He smiles when we break apart, and I turn away to hide my emotion. It's been too long since we did that, and it makes my eyes well up with tears.

Archie and Charles finish unloading the car before joining us.

"Where shall I put the bags, Mrs. Ainsworth?" Archie asks.

"I've told you before, please call me Edith." She hugs Archie. "I've given you and Victoria the downstairs room, so you'll have a little more privacy."

"We only have one room?" I ask, trying to hide my shock.

"Don't worry, it's as big as the one in your apartment, and there's a downstairs bathroom." My mum reads my lack of enthusiasm wrong. I guess couples would usually share a room, but if we'd had our own lodge, Archie and I could have had a bed each.

"Thanks, Edith," Archie says, heading down the hall to find it. I follow him and close the door once all our bags are inside.

"I'm so sorry about this," I say, eyeing up the double bed.

"It's okay. I can sleep on the sofa," he says.

"That's not big enough for a grown man to sleep on. We're both adults. We can share the bed." I pat the duvet.

"Whatever you want is cool with me." He places his bag on the sofa and walks over to the window.

It's more about what I don't want. Archie would be at home in his comfy bed if I hadn't dragged him here. He's a nice guy and a gentleman. We may have started out with a bad connection, but I like him, and if I give it a chance, I think we could be friends.

We unpack and join my family for a meal cooked by one of Cornwall's finest chefs, Pierre Walters. The snack I ate early probably wasn't a good idea, but if it makes Archie see me as a little normal I can't regret it.

In between courses, I step outside. My dad opens the patio doors, and we stand together on the decking, waiting for dessert. The lights are on in the holiday homes, and I stare out into the night. The place looks pretty in the dark as the icicles twinkle.

"Are all the lodges full?" I ask to break the silence.

"Yes. Most of our good friends are here." He leans against the balcony. It's been a long time since we were under one roof, and it feels a little strange.

"It's nice to see you." I twist my fingers together. I don't want to say the wrong thing.

"You look beautiful. I'm glad you're looking after yourself." A ghost of a smile crosses his face.

"Thank you." That's the nicest thing he's said to me in a long time, and he seems to be trying to mend bridges.

He lets out a deep breath while looking off into the distance. "I'm glad you came. It means a lot to your mother... and me."

"Mum's being secretive. Are you going to tell me what's going on?"

He wraps his arm around my shoulders. I tense at first but then relax. Tears threaten for the second time tonight. I've waited for us to be close for such a long time that a simple hug is overwhelming. "It's all good. I promise. For a while, I thought you were too wrapped up in your work to find a partner. It's nice to see you've found a man," he says, gesturing to Archie, who is playing FIFA with my brother. My breath hitches. There's so much I want to say, but I have to start by explaining I haven't changed my stance on marriage.

"Not everyone needs to find someone to settle down with." I brace my hands together, squeezing them tightly. *Please don't be angry that I've shared my thoughts.*

"No, but you don't realise what you're missing out on until it's too late." He sounds sad, and it makes me pause. I'm not sure what loss makes my dad feel this way, and maybe I'll never find out, but I wish I could ease his pain.

Seeing my brother and Archie battle it out on the games console gives me a warm, fuzzy feeling. Usually, the guys I've dated have been serious, and Charles is a free spirit. He never took enough time to drink a whole cup of coffee with any of them. Tonight, those two have been playing on the console between courses. The feeling amongst my family is happier than usual, and it warms my heart. "Yes. I understand what you mean. I have my work, but some nights can be lonely." I smile cheerlessly.

"Have you thought about moving in with Archie?"

My eyes widen. I'm surprised he's accepting Archie so easily, but also disappointed his heart's set on me settling down. I'm not annoyed, though. It's a simple enough question and I want to try to mend our relationship. "It's too soon for that." When I get back to London, maybe I will consider dating again. Archie is making me crave things I didn't know I wanted.

"The tiramisu cheesecake is ready," my mother says.

Dad pats me on the back before holding the door for

me to step through.

We all move back to the table, and I sit next to my fake boyfriend. "Your game looked intense," I say.

"Your brother doesn't like to lose." He smiles.

"At least I know how to win," Charles says.

"We'll see."

They start laughing and I shake my head. "How old are you both?" I joke.

"Aww, don't spoil our fun. We're only messing around. You've finally brought a boyfriend home that I like and I'm not allowed to play with him." Charles pouts.

"Did you think my previous boyfriends were so bad?" I frown.

"Yes," Charles and my dad say at the same time.

"I liked Benedict from school," Mum says.

"Especially him," Dad adds.

"You liked his money," Charles says.

"He did have good heritage," Mum agrees.

"I liked his looks. Victoria and Benedict would've made good-looking babies. But I see we don't have to worry about that. Our Victoria likes the pretty ones." My aunt fans her face like she's having a hot flush.

Everyone is quiet for a few seconds before they burst

out laughing.

"Yes. Archie is ten times the man Benedict will ever be," I say boldly. It's strange I'm already sticking up for him, even though I barely know him. In my heart, I know my words are true. He seems to be caring and passionate about the things he wants. He has qualities I like in a person and I'm not afraid to praise him.

"Aww, that's cute. I propose a toast to Victoria and Archie. May their children be beautiful," my aunt says.

Everyone takes a drink.

My cheeks warm. "We haven't dated that long. Let's see if we make it to the new year first."

"Why wouldn't you make it to January?" my mum asks, louder than needed.

"Stop teasing your mum, Victoria. We're doing just

fine… unless there's something you need to tell me?"

Archie puts his hand over mine and everyone is

looking intently at us.

I smile. "No. Everything is going perfectly."

Archie leans in and places a soft kiss on my cheek. Wow. This is what a relationship is supposed to be like. My face is hot, I have butterflies in my stomach, and the only thing wrong is that it's not real.

Faking it with Archie

CHAPTER NINE

Archie sleeps peacefully, and I can't help thinking this is another perfect thing about him. He doesn't snore or hog the bed. Slowly, I ease myself out from underneath the duvet and creep towards the door.

I find my mum boiling the kettle in the kitchen area.

"Morning," I say, grabbing a cup from the stand.

"Morning. Did you sleep well?" She adds a teabag to my cup.

"Like a princess." *The Princess and the Pea* was one of my favourite stories. In the book, the princess has a rough night. Since I didn't have peas in my bed, I slept well. We used to say this all the time when I was younger. It made my mum smile like it does now.

Memories of spending Christmas abroad come flooding back. Charles and I used to spend the weeks skiing, exploring, or surfing. I used to sleep peacefully because I was so exhausted from the fun days out. Now I wake up early and work late. Maybe this holiday was what I needed.

"I thought we could go into town today and look at the local handmade treasures while the men prepare for the hog roast in the barn for tonight."

"Yes, that sounds great." I used to love shopping with my mum when I was younger and I'm feeling sentimental.

We make pancakes and sausages. The smell must awaken the whole house. By the time we've finished, everyone is sitting at the table, drinking coffee.

I sit next to Archie, who looks like he stepped off the cover of Gallant rather than just crawled out of bed.

"Morning, beautiful," he says as I put our plates of food down on the table.

"Morning, handsome." We smile at each other, and for a second, I almost believe the lie.

"You'd already fallen asleep before I finished the game with your brother last night."

"I needed my beauty sleep. I hadn't realised how exhausted I was until my head hit the pillow." I cut off a small piece of my pancake and put it into my mouth. The syrup awakens my taste buds. "I'm going to go shopping with the ladies this morning, but we'll catch up after lunch. Will you be okay?"

"Of course he will. We have a barn to prepare, and I

need a FIFA rematch," Charles says.

"We have all week together. We'll find time for each other." Archie winks at me, and the urge to kiss him comes out of nowhere. Instead, I fill my mouth with another fork full of pancake.

After the food, everyone goes to their rooms to get ready.

"Do you want to shower first?" I ask Archie once we're alone.

"No, you go ahead. I want to call my mum."

"Thanks." I step into the bathroom and close the door. When I'm washed and changed, I find Archie sitting on the bed in a towel. I avoid staring and move over to the dresser. "The shower's all yours." I apply my foundation as he disappears out of the room.

I'm almost ready by the time Archie reappears from the bathroom. "Will you fasten this?" I ask him, holding out my wrist with my bracelet resting over it.

"Sure." He towers over me as he moves in close.

"Sorry I have to leave you this morning." He seems to like my brother, so I'm mainly apologising out of courtesy.

His eyes meet mine. "It's no problem. I want you to enjoy yourself and I'm here whenever you need me." The way he says it makes it sound seductive.

My tongue darts out to wet my dry lips. I really want to kiss him, but I break eye contact instead. "I'm not sure what I expected when I brought you here. You're making this very easy, though. My family loves you already."

"They're all great. You're lucky to have them. I needed the money, which is part of the reason I decided to come, but I also wanted to get to know you."

I try to hide the happy smile that's bursting to get out. "Don't worry. I'll make sure you're in my spring collection."

"It's not just that."

"Then why?" Our friendship didn't get off to a good start. Why would he want to give me another chance to get to know him on a personal level?

"I like your ambition. It's attractive. Once I had a taste of what you're really about, I couldn't stop thinking about you."

"Is this some plot to get me back for messing with your career?" Archie's compliments are hard to accept, and I'm waiting for him to say it was a joke or something. It's been a long time since I cared what someone thought about me, but I do care what he thinks.

He laughs softly before dragging his teeth along his bottom lip. "Nope. I'm serious about getting to know you. Being part of your fashion team would be a nice bonus too."

Our eyes meet again. My lips part, and we start to lean

in close. A knock at the door interrupts us and we stop in our tracks.

"Are you ready?" my mum shouts through the door.

"Almost," I shout back. "I'd better go before she comes in here."

"Until later then." He kisses my cheek. The place his lips touched my face feels warm. I rise my hand to trace the outline. He watches me, and I struggle to break eye contact.

"See you soon."

"Goodbye."

I step out into the hall and follow my mum out to the seventeen-seater minibus. The Winter Lodges has its own transportation for hire and the owner agreed to take us to the nearest town. My head is fuzzy from Archie's confession. He was flirting with me, and I liked it. When I saw him at the office, I instantly knew he was my type and that hiring him would only intensify my attraction. It's not just about his looks, though. He's charming, and even though I wasn't looking for a boyfriend, he's making me reconsider.

"Morning," Isabella Lorelson says as I walk to my seat.

"Good morning. Thank you for returning my dress." I touch the headrest of the seat she's sitting on and stop to talk.

"I hope you don't mind, but I wore it to the winter

dance."

"Not at all. I hope you enjoyed wearing it." My smile beams with pride.

"I did." She cups her hand into a heart.

Isabella is sitting with her mum, and I acknowledge her with a friendly greeting. "Morning, Mrs Lorelson."

"Morning, Victoria. It's nice to see you again."

"You too." Instead of lingering for longer, I move on. Isabella enjoyed wearing my dress and that's enough for now. I take the compliment and store it on my mental achievement shelf.

I greet a few more ladies, including Regena, as I walk up the aisle to take the seat next to my mum. I'm excited for this trip. Other than work days out, this is the most sociable I've been in ages. It's a short journey to the nearest town, and I enjoy the scenery while chatting with my mum.

"I'm going to look at the art shops," I say.

"That sounds fun. What kind of painting or handmade trinket would you like?" Her eyes light up as she rubs her hands together.

"A snowy picture of Cornwall will look great in my office. It will remind me of this trip." I can already picture it on my plain white wall.

"That sounds like a lovely idea. I might get one too." We make a plan to find the best art shops, and it isn't long until we arrive at our destination. We spend the next few hours shopping and each of us buys a small painting. I get some last-minute gifts, and we lunch in a local deli. It feels good to enjoy a relaxing day with my mum.

"We have one more stop before we go back to the lodge." My mum leads us down a narrow path towards the outskirts of the town centre.

"Okay." We all follow until we reach a bridal shop. "What's going on?" I ask curiously.

"Your father and I are going to renew our vows on Christmas Eve." My mum's hands shake with excitement.

"Congrats. If I'd known, I would've packed a dress for the occasion." Visions of dresses I've made and could have made flash through my head.

The group of ladies offers their best wishes.

"Congrats," Lucy Lorelson says.

"That's amazing," another friend says.

"Thanks, everyone," Mum says before turning her attention to me. "I wanted to keep it as a surprise. I have a dress picked out for you."

If she'd given me notice, I could've made the perfect outfit. I could've... then it hits me. She didn't want me to make my own outfit, but why? Hurt and confusion wash over me. Did my mum want me to have a relaxing time instead of fussing over my design? Did she want to surprise us with the news, or is there something deeper going on here? "How come you're telling me now?"

"I've kept it a secret for as long as I could. Come inside, everyone, so you can see my dress." She gestures to the door of the bridal shop.

I'm slow to let my happiness show. I can see this means a lot to herm and maybe me wearing what she's chosen is important to her. We go inside, and I try on the simple ruby red gown. It's plain and classy. When I come out of the changing room, I get a round of compliments. The dress is lovely. There's a nice atmosphere in the air and it feels good to be part of it. We're all talking and drinking prosecco by the time my mum is ready.

"Wow. You look beautiful," I say. Her dress is vintage and elegant. It's similar to the ruby red one I have on, only with embroidered detail across the hem.

"Thank you." We hug each other.

Some of the women try on a few outfits from the mother of the bride rail, and I can't help thinking I could've made everyone's outfits. Has my mother stopped inviting me to balls and events because I can't leave my work at home? I'm happy for her, but we need to talk about what's been going on. Do I take over when I have my business head on?

Archie was furious when I didn't give him the modelling job, and again when I let my ambition overrule my morals. Looking back, maybe I should've tried to convince my boss Archie was worth fighting for. I could've tried to find a new angle to work his campaign. I feel bad about the way I let him down. Instead of dwelling on the details for too long, I try to enjoy this moment.

We try on bridal shoes and jewellery. There are some interesting designs, and I enjoy playing fashion show.

"I hope someday soon I'll get to do this all again with you for your wedding," Mum says as we look in the mirror together.

It isn't that I don't want to get married, but it's hard to predict the future when you're not sure if your fake boyfriend is someone you'd like to date for real. "I'm sorry we fell out when I chose a career over a husband," I say.

"Your father and I only wanted the best for you. Alexander would've been a good match. I'm sorry we didn't realise you were unhappy." She rubs my shoulder, and I pull her into a hug.

I'm glad she's opening up to me, and I regret not doing this sooner. We need to talk about this. "Do you think Dad will forgive me eventually?"

"He handled the situation badly, but he loves you. I'm sure you'll make up."

This Christmas feels different. Dad and I have spoken more in the last two days than we have in years. "I hope so."

"I want us to have more family time when we get home." We break apart but stay close.

"I'd like that." I smile widely.

She rubs my arm, offering comfort. "I would too. I've missed you."

"Me too."

She blinks back tears. "The distance between us is all in the past now. I only want you to be happy."

"Can I ask you something while we're being truthful? What is it about my designs that makes you avoid them?" I bite my lip, hoping I've not been too outspoken.

"What do you mean?"

"If I'd known I needed a formal dress for our trip, I would've made one."

She rubs the edge of her collar, casting her eyes down for a few seconds. She looks guilty as she meets my gaze once more. "Your designs are stunning. I'm very proud of your work. The problem is the time it takes up. When I call, you're working. When I ask you to meet me for coffee, you're too busy with your designs, and when I want to do something with you, you're always trying to figure out how it will benefit your career. I want to spend time with my daughter. When I saw you were dating Archie, I thought finally you'd found something more for your life. My dad wasn't around much when I was younger, and he brought nice things back from his business trips, but what I really wanted was to spend time with him. I don't want that future for you." She's presuming I want children, and I do, one day. She's never talked about her father like this, and it will take time to process, but the meaning isn't lost on me.

I nod, fighting back tears. I understand what she's saying. It'll be nice to have her in my life more, and I intend to clear my schedule to make it happen. "I love you, Mum."

"I love you too." We hug each other again, only tighter.

Once the dresses and accessories are parcelled up, we head back into town. Something between us already feels different. I can't control my smile. It's like a weight has been lifted off my shoulders, and I feel lighter. We enjoy the rest of our trip and arrive home in time for the evening festivities.

We shower and change before meeting the guys in the barn. I hang my thick white coat on a peg near the door. My red winter dress hugs my figure, and I catch Archie staring as I enter the room. I wave as I approach the table he's sitting at.

"Hello," I say.

"Evening. You look beautiful. Did you have a good day?" He stands and kisses my cheek before helping me into a seat. His lips feel great against my skin. Warmth spreads from my belly, and my eyes linger on his.

"You look great too," I say. He's wearing a black turtleneck and dark jeans. It suits him, like everything he wears, but my compliment goes deeper than his clothes. The smile on his lips and the kindness in his eyes are genuinely mesmerizing.

Everyone staying at the Winter Lodges makes their way to sit with us at the giant oak table. My dad is wearing a Father Christmas cooking apron and serves the meat from the small counter area at the back of the barn. In small groups, we all go to collect our food.

"Thank you," I say as I hold my plate out for him to put the turkey on.

"You're welcome," Dad says as he serves me.

"I love the outfit," I say, pointing at his apron. It says *Kiss the Chef* under Santa's beard.

"Maybe next year I'll get you one." He laughs. I like seeing him like this.

"I'd like that." Having a stronger connection to my dad is what I want, even if it's just matching novelty aprons. "Congrats on the vow renewal ceremony."

He taps my arm in a comforting way. "It's for your mother. Whatever makes her happy."

The love my mum and dad share is inspirational. They support each other through thick and thin. It's lovely. I understand why my parents value marriage and why they wanted that for me too. I want to repair the rift between us more than anything.

Archie helps my dad by serving the vegetables before getting his own food. Once everyone has what they need, Archie sits next to me to eat.

David Lorelson sits at my other side. "Evening," he says.

"Hi. Are you enjoying Cornwall?" I ask.

"Yes. It's good to escape the office."

"It sure is." For the first time, I actually mean this. It isn't a cliché line I've said just because I'm supposed to. As I look around the table, there isn't a better group of people I'd rather spend my time with. If I'd stayed at my apartment, I would've been missing out.

"I promised my wife I wouldn't talk about work, so I'll keep this brief. I'd like you to consider helping Isabella with her birthday party."

A few days ago, I'd have relished the chance to discuss work. Now, I think his wife has it right. That doesn't mean I want to miss an opportunity, though. My mum mentioned he intended to talk to me. I like Isabella, and I want to help her any way I can.

"I'd love to be part of the celebration, whatever she has in mind. Have her ring my office in the new year and I'll get my assistant to set up a meeting so we can discuss the details."

"That's wonderful news. Thanks."

I enjoy my meal, making small talk with Archie and David. We keep talk of fashion to a minimum and laugh about bad Christmas presents.

"Shall we take a walk?" Archie asks after the food.

"Yes. Let me grab my coat," I say.

Leaving everyone at the table, I find my coat hanging on one of the pegs. Archie strolls over, meeting me at the doorway.

"How was shopping with your mum?" he asks.

We step out into the cold, and I pull my hood up. The temperature has dropped now the winter sun has gone in. The outside air is crisp, and I can see my breath in front of my face.

"Good, thanks. Did my brother tell you my mum and dad are renewing their vows on Christmas Eve?"

He rubs his arms. "Yes. He told me not to say anything because your mum wanted it to be a surprise."

"She said today she wanted to keep it a secret as long as possible, but did everyone know apart from me?" I frown.

"Your brother only told me yesterday, and I think everyone else found out today. I was told so your brother could order the men's suits to be delivered. He needed my measurements." He hugs himself, shivering.

"Shall we call at the lodge and get your coat?"

"Yes. I think that's a good idea." We head towards our holiday home.

"After talking to my mum today, I'm beginning to think my work is getting in the way of my family life." The icicle and candy cane lights sparkle, brightening the night sky.

"What do you mean?"

"Until today, I thought my mum didn't support my career because I didn't marry the man she picked for me, but now I'm wondering if some of the decisions I've made have put a wedge between us too. When I'm invited to a party, I try to promote my designs. Maybe it's too much. Maybe my mum's been keeping me away from her friends because I can't leave my work at home."

We reach the lodge, and Archie grabs his coat before we head out for our walk. He's quiet for a few minutes, probably trying to find the right words. "Your work is important to you, but maybe you can balance it with some fun." He sounds respectful, like he doesn't want to offend me. Also, I'm getting the impression he agrees with my mum on some level.

"Do you think I'm a workaholic?" As soon as the words are out of my mouth, I know the truth. I shake my head. "Actually, you don't need to answer that. Be honest with me. After the way I treated you, why did you agree to come here with me?" I change my question. I wonder what Archie sees when he looks at me. Am I too driven to stop and take a second to enjoy the beauty around me?

We continue into the woodland area, away from the bright lights. The path is dark, and we slow our pace so we can watch our steps. Archie takes a deep breath. "I went to the ball in the hope of ruining your night."

"What?" My eyes widen in surprise. Archie is so nice; I can't imagine him sabotaging anything.

He shrugs. "That was probably childish of me. I thought if I could wreck your evening, I'd feel better about you not choosing me. Then your mother was so lovely, and I could see you were having problems with working the room, so I couldn't go through with it."

I hold my stomach. If I'd followed my heart instead of my head, he would've been hired straight away. My hesitation could've cost me greatly, even though I wouldn't have known it. I'm glad Archie allowed me to get to know him. "You're right. I should've chosen you from the beginning. I only chose Lloyd because I wasn't attracted to him." This probably isn't the best time to confess my feelings, but I want to get everything out in the open.

"That's the dumbest reason I've ever heard. I thought something was off. That's why I followed you out into the hall. I'd done my research on the company, and when I saw Lloyd, I thought I would've easily got the job. You crushed my spirit a little that day." He clutches his chest, pretending to show his emotional wound.

"I'm sorry for that. It wasn't my intention." I frown. Archie's taught me to be a better person, and although not everyone in life is nice, I'm going to try to give people a fair shot.

He stops and puts his hand against my heart. "You should start thinking with this instead of your head."

I nod. I do need to start using my feelings rather than my head or I'm going to push everyone away. "Can we start over as friends?"

Archie shakes his head. "That's just a cliche line people say. We can't go back to that day. We can only have a better relationship from now."

"How did you become so wise?" Without thinking about it too hard, I lean and give him a hug. Melanie and I would do this if we had a heart-to-heart or a disagreement. Being close to Archie feels different, though. It feels great to be in his arms; maybe a little too great. My heart flutters with. Archie affects me in a way I never thought anyone would. He's so warm and friendly. The crush I had on him at the beginning was superficial, based upon his looks alone, but the man is also stunning on the inside.

"Trust me, I've made enough of my own mistakes."

"Maybe I need to hear some of these stories."

He laughs. "I don't think we're there yet. I might scare you off."

We smile at each other. I'm happy we have cleared the air. Eventually, I hope he'll share with me, and his tales can't be that bad. "It's good we'll be working together for a while, then. We have the spring collection, and maybe I can find you a bathing suit for summer." I playfully wink at him.

"There's just one problem. I don't think you're supposed to fancy your boss." He smiles cheekily.

"You like me?" I ask, even though he already told me he did.

"We almost kissed this morning. Of course I like you."

He starts to lean in towards my lips, but I stop him. "This might be another stupid decision, but I think we should wait. We can date and work together, as long as we're professional in the office. First, I need to prove I can put someone before my work."

He nods, accepting my decision. "I look forward to seeing what you have in store."

"Me too."

We walk back to the barn, and although we didn't get our first kiss, we enjoy our night together.

CHAPTER TEN

"Who's up for a game of Charades?" Archie asks, pulling out the box from under the coffee table.

"I'm stuffed from the Christmas pudding. I'm not sure I can move," my aunt says, patting her tummy. My mum made another amazing dinner, but all this rich food is sending me into a coma. I've eaten too much too, so I understand what she means.

"Come on. Don't let the girls' side down," my mum says. She sits on the sofa next to me, already deciding who will be on her team.

"I bet Archie's like a pool shark. I'm happy to be on his team," Charles says.

"I hope you enjoy losing," I answer. Laughter and idle threats break out in the group.

"Is everyone happy with boys vs girls?" Archie asks.

"It's been a long time since I was called a boy," my dad says, making everyone laugh.

"Men vs women," my brother says, too enthusiastically for me to argue with him. He playfully pushes me as he stands up to move to the other sofa.

We split into teams and Archie sets up the game. "It's Christmas themed, and in the spirit of good fun, I think it's fair we let the ladies go first."

"I need wine," my aunt says. I get up so I can retrieve the bottle from the kitchen and top up her glass.

"While you're on your feet. You can go first," Archie says.

I frown. "Aww, thanks. I thought you were on my side."

"Not right now," he says with a wink.

I pick a card while giving him the evil eye. Without showing anyone, I look at the word. *Snowman. How on earth am I going to do this?*

Everyone's staring at me, and I'm frozen to the spot.

"And go," Archie says. He turns over the sand timer.

Pretending to roll a ball, I start to build an imaginary snowman.

"Circus," Mum shouts.

"Dog," my aunt chips in.

They keep guessing wrong, and my brother laughs.

"Don't forget it's Christmas-related," Archie says. He's smiling but not quite laughing.

I take off my fake scarf and wrap it around my snowman. I do the same with imaginary gloves.

"Christmas dog," my aunt says.

I swat my head.

"You're almost out of time," Charles says.

"Come on." I throw my hands down in frustration before putting a hat on the head of my pretend snowman.

"You lose," Charles says.

"You guys what else wears a hat, scarf, and gloves other than a snowman?" I ask, shaking my head at my family.

"I knew what it was," Archie says.

I flick my hand at him. "See!"

"Don't be a sore loser," Charles says. He goes next, and Archie guesses ice skating in less than a minute.

I roll up my sleeves. "We have to get this one."

My mum stands and looks at the card nervously. She starts to dance. It looks like an Irish jig. I look at my aunt, and she shrugs.

"We're doomed." I cover my head with my hands.

"Christmas dog," my aunt guesses again, and I start laughing. We both laugh until our time is almost over.

"Ooh, Christmas elf," I say, jumping up.

My mum claps. "Got it."

The game continues, and I fiercely try to keep up with the men, who are so much better at this.

"Victory is ours," Charles says as we close the last round. Even my dad cheers, and he doesn't usually like playing games.

I shake my head. "Next time, we're making the teams unisex."

My brother goes on to tell us about some of his adventures. It's nice to see him and learn about where he's been. I envy his free spirit. My parents have always supported whatever he wanted to do, and it spikes an ounce of jealousy within me. I wish I could hike in the Australian outback or swim with dolphins in the ocean. It would be nice to have stories to tell that my parents were interested in.

We're still laughing and joking as Archie and I head to our room.

"I'm sorry you lost at Charades."

"You were a little traitor," I joke, playfully pushing him to the wall. This is the sort of behaviour I'd use with my brother, but it's different with Archie. It's flirty.

"Hey. If you damage my good looks, you'll be sorry."

"You'll have to become a hand model or something."

"Very funny."

He holds the door open so I can enter the bedroom first. I get my pyjamas on in the bathroom and brush my teeth. Once Archie is ready, he joins me in the bed.

"You looked beautiful tonight," he says as we stare at each other.

"I was only wearing an oversized jumper and leggings." I smile. He's such a charmer.

"Your outfit wasn't what I was talking about. Relaxing with your family in the lodge brings out the best in you."

Warmth fills my chest. "I wouldn't call Charades relaxing. Didn't you see me screaming with frustration?"

"Just take the compliment," he says, turning away so he can switch off the light.

"Thank you." I snuggle into the duvet.

He lies on his back, facing the ceiling.

After a few minutes, I say, "I hope you're having a nice Christmas."

"I am."

"Me too."

After a longer pause, he says, "Goodnight."

"Sweet dreams."

I've had a fun night and I can't wait to do more with my family and Archie. If every Christmas was like this, I may consider naming it my favourite holiday.

CHAPTER ELEVEN

The next few days pass, and I enjoy spending time with my family. We play board games and take walks in the woods. My sketch pad never leaves my bag, and I try to be in the moment. Archie is a dream, and I've forgotten why I resisted him the other night.

"We're going to head into town to watch a show," my mum says.

"We thought you and Archie could enjoy a night alone," my brother adds with a wink.

"You're all going?" I ask.

"It's my Christmas present to your mum and dad. I didn't know if you were going to make the trip, and your brother booked his own ticket," my aunt says.

"Oh." I understand she didn't realise I was coming when she bought the tickets. However, if I'd been told earlier, I might've got us tickets too, but it would be nice to have some time alone with Archie.

"I could try and get you two seats if you want to come?" Charles says.

"No. It's okay." I look at Archie. "Unless you want to go?"

"No. I'm sure we can think of something to do."

Thirty minutes later, we're left alone for the first time since we arrived at the Winter Lodges.

"What do you want to do?" I ask.

Archie raises an eyebrow with a smirk. "I can think of a few things."

I shake my head. "Hot chocolate and a Christmas movie?"

"That's so PG 13." He waves his hands, signalling that it's not going to happen.

I laugh. "Okay, so what do you have in mind?"

"Festive cocktails and *The Big Fat Quiz of the Year*." He rubs his hands together.

I like seeing him all fired up, and he seems committed to making this fun. I'm not against the idea, but unless he knows someone with inside knowledge, we can't watch something that hasn't been broadcast. "Is that on TV tonight? I thought it wasn't on until Boxing Day?"

"The day varies every year, but I don't think it's been

on yet. I'll find last year's show." He shrugs.

That's an easy solution. "I probably watched it. I may have an advantage." I'm teasing him because my memory isn't good enough to remember a quiz show from twelve months ago.

"I know you don't like to lose, so I'm okay with that."

I hold my hands up. "I'm just offering a full disclosure."

"Oh, you never give everything away." He smiles playfully. "I probably watched it too, but I can't remember what I had for breakfast yesterday, so I doubt a quiz show I watched a year ago is going to come flooding back."

"But you know how to make a festive cocktail?"

"Of course. If I wasn't here with you, I'd be working in a London bar right now."

"Okay, show me your mad skills." I gesture to the kitchen.

He rolls up his sleeves and leads the way. He raids the cupboards for the ingredients he needs and sets me the task of squeezing the lime.

When he's finished, he passes me the cocktail. "What do you think?"

I take a sip. "Mmm, delicious. What's it called?"

"It's a cranberry margarita, courtesy of the BBC Goodfood website."

After we've finished, Archie makes a jug of cocktail mix to top up our glasses. We take our drinks into the living space, and he finds *The Big Fat Quiz of the Year*. I grab some pens and paper from my room and we set up, ready for the quiz. We sit on opposite sofas, and I poise my pen, ready for action.

The first round is easy, and we both score five points.

I fill my glass back up. "I'm going to take you down in this round."

"I don't think so." He shakes his head.

The host starts the questions, and I focus on my paper. We both get the same question wrong in this round, keeping the score even. The cocktail is going down too easily, and I start to feel lightheaded. "Is the plan to get me drunk and then hope I slip up?"

"You're the one drinking it." He fills his glass. He tilts it to his lips, watching me, and the liquid smoothly glides down his throat. He finishes it and puts the empty glass on the table.

The next question comes on, and I get ready to write down the answer. Archie's still watching me. "What?" I ask.

"I like you when you're like this."

"Tipsy?" I giggle.

"Relaxed." He smiles lazily.

"Cocktails and a quiz were a great idea. I'll have to hire you for the New Year celebration too." I'm kind of joking. Archie is great company, and spending more time with him would be fantastic. When I'm home alone, surrounded by my work, I only have the TV as a companion. Sometimes, my apartment does seem too quiet, but I didn't realise I was lonely until I met him. Now I'm seeing the advantage of having someone. It's nice to be silly and fun. Winding down and letting someone in isn't as scary as I thought it would be. Being able to relax is something that's been missing from my life, and I want more of everything I've had on this trip. More time with family and more opportunities to enjoy people in general.

"Why? What do you normally do?"

"Usually, I drag my assistant to the firework display near the London Eye, but this year, she's spending it with her family." The buzz of the people in the capital is electric. My assistant is my best friend and we enjoy doing things together. She's always there when I need her, but she has her own life and family. Our relationship is changing, and I need to evolve. I've never had a boyfriend for the occasion, and a kiss at midnight sounds magical. Archie is making me want someone who is mine and going home with me at the end of the night. A friendship is no longer enough. His kindness and charm make my heart beat to a new rhythm.

"You wouldn't have to pay me to hang out with you."

My cheeks flame. I shouldn't have to rent a date for company, but it does make it easier. "Won't you be working New Year?"

"Not if we have plans."

Butterflies erupt in my stomach. The next question comes on the TV, and I turn to face it. Archie stands and moves towards me. I jump up from the sofa, meeting his gaze before he can sit next to me. I start to feel light-headed, like I'm going to pass out, and it's not from getting up too fast. His gaze is so intense I know something big is about to happen.

"What are you doing?" His arms wrap around me, and he pulls me close. His lips crash down on mine, and I'm slow to respond.

Archie has always kept me on my toes, and even though I've been trying to resist him, I can't do it this time. My lips begin to move with his, and our tongues massage each other's. He deepens the kiss, and I'm more than eager to follow his lead. It's hot as hell. I've never been kissed like this before. A moan leaves my mouth, making my face heat. It's passionate and makes me feel flustered. I break away from him to try and compose myself.

"You have some skills." *Just don't use them to break my heart.* I probably shouldn't have said that out loud, but I guess it was better than thanking him or something else more awkward.

"It can't be that good if you're running away."

"I'm just getting ready for the next round." Collecting my notepad, I take a seat and gulp down a large mouthful of my cranberry margarita. I need a breather before I embarrass myself. If I was a guy, I'd be sporting a hard-on.

"Okay, if that's how you want to play it." He sits back on his sofa. His cheeks are rosy, but the corners of his mouth pull down. Did I upset him? It wasn't my intention to make things uncomfortable. The possibility of us having a relationship is new and I don't want to rush into it.

My stomach tightens. I hope I haven't hurt his feelings or ruined anything. I hate seeing him disappointed. God, I'm a mess. I haven't been this bad since submitting my dissertation, when I had to pick my strongest designs for my portfolio. Focusing on the TV, I try to block him out. I need to deal with my feelings before I make it worse between us.

We finish the quiz, but my win seems empty. "That was an interesting set of questions," I say.

"Well done on the win." He clears the glasses into the kitchen area. The vibe between us is a little strange.

"Thanks." I follow him to the sink. I've had too much to drink and I'm wobbly on my feet. He washes up in the sink before drying his hands on the towel. I linger for a few seconds, but I'm not ready to talk about us. "What are you doing now? I'm sleepy, so I'm going to go to bed."

He studies me for a moment. "A quick game on FIFA sounds good to me." Gently, he taps the countertop before heading back into the living space. He turns on the console, collecting his controller.

He seems to realise I need some time to clear my thoughts, and I do, although I wish he was coming to lie next to me. "Okay. Goodnight."

The door to the lodge opens and my family noisily comes in.

"All I'm saying is, if you got rid of the Christmas lights, you could rename this place the Summer Lodges and it would have holidaymakers queuing up," Charles says.

"That's probably what they do anyway. They wouldn't even need to take the icicles down from the roof. They could just switch them off." They hang their coats up and remove their shoes.

"Hi. How was the theatre?" I say with an over-the-top smile. I'd rather they didn't know something has happened with Archie because I don't need them to interfere.

"Amazing," Charlies says. He grabs a bottle of beer out of the fridge and uses the bottle opener from the drawer to remove the lid. After retrieving a joypad, he sits down next to Archie.

"Wine?" Mum asks as she goes into the kitchen. My aunt follows her and retrieves some glasses from the cupboard. My dad warms his hands on the radiator. All their faces are red from the cold, but only my dad seems to be suffering.

"No, thanks. It's late and I'm tired, so I'm going to bed." I hug my mum and kiss my aunt's cheek. I leave the room without looking back at Archie.

"Is everything okay?" my dad asks in the hall with a frown. He's followed me, so maybe me rushing off seemed out of character.

"Yes. I'm a little drunk and ready to lie down." I kiss him goodnight. My dad and I need to talk more, but I'm glad he easily accepts my affection.

Once alone, I take off my make-up and crawl into bed. I feel bad for the way the night ended, and I can't sleep. I spend the next two hours staring at the ceiling while listening to the noises in the lodge. When Archie comes to bed, I pretend to be in a deep slumber. The bed dips when he climbs in.

More time passes, and I'm still wide awake. Archie's arm moves over me, and he pulls me close. I'm stiff at first, unsure if he's awake. Instead of questioning what's happening, I enjoy the comfort and finally start to drift off.

CHAPTER TWELVE

Christmas Eve arrives too quickly, and my parents are renewing their vows today. Archie and I haven't spoken about what happened the night we kissed. The tension between us has been weird for the past forty-eight hours. He's been gaming with my brother, and I've been pottering around. At night, we've said pleasantries, but it's just not us. Even though I feel bad about it, I can't bring myself to mention it because… what if he rejects me? We'd both been drinking that night, and I'm not good at talking about my problems.

We sit in the barn, waiting for my mum to arrive. There are close friends and family around us, and I finally understand why this was so important to my mum. They've been married for twenty-five years, and having everyone here feels special.

"Do you think we can be friends and talk about the black cloud in the room later?" I ask Archie.

"I'm not sure I know what you mean."

I touch his arm. "I'm sorry if I've hurt your feelings. It wasn't my intention."

He stares at me. His expression is serious, and I'm not sure what he's going to say. "I'm angry. Initially, I was hurt, but I realised something."

I guess we're going to talk about this now. I bite my lip, hoping this doesn't get out of hand. He's not the only one with heightened emotions. I squeeze my fist to add to my discomfort. I'm angry too, even though it's myself I'm blaming. "What did you realise?"

"You like me." His grimace tightens. He doesn't seem happy about his discovery.

"I…"

We're interrupted by Regena, my mum's friend, who sits in the chair next to Archie. "Hello. You both look stunning. Are they your designs, Victoria?" She smiles, and Archie unclenches his jaw.

"I got it from the bridal shop when we visited town, remember?" I force out a smile, trying not to be rude. I don't want her here right now when I could be sorting out my relationship.

"Oh, yes. Sorry. It's just, you always look beautiful."

The dress my mum picked out is lovely. The red looks beautiful against my pale skin. "Thanks. You look good too," I say. She's wearing a dusky pink dress with an A-line skirt.

"Thanks." She pulls her fuchsia shawl up onto her shoulders. "So, Archie, when are you going to make an honest woman out of her?"

He freezes, and I think he's not going to answer at first. "Maybe one day... if she's lucky." He whispers something in her ear, and Regena throws her head back to let out a laugh.

What is so funny?

"And do you want children?" she asks.

"Yes, ma'am. I do."

They both turn to me. "Sure." I nod, feeling under pressure and wishing they'd both look away.

"The more the merrier," Archie says. He doesn't smile, and it feels like we're still arguing.

Luckily, Regena gets the hint and moves on. "Excuse me. I think I see an old friend." She rushes off far away from us.

There's chatter around us, and no one is paying attention to our conversation. I want to try and smooth things out between us. I want to understand him on a personal level without causing a scene. Asking about his future family plans probably isn't the safest topic, but Regena did already give me an opening.

"What do you call big? A football team's worth?" I try to lighten the conversation.

"No. Not that many. I was thinking three or four."

He doesn't smile, and I want to pull his face up into a cheeky grin.

"That's a lot of children. The park mums will love you. They'll be drooling all over you. I can just see it now. Three mini versions of you running around with a football. You teaching all the kids on the field how to spin a ball on their finger." I try again to cheer his mood, but I'm rambling.

"That's basketball you're thinking of. It's a shame you're not smitten enough to admit you care about me." He frowns before turning away.

My breath hitches, but I can't completely shut down or I'll push him further away. I reach out and put my hand on his arm. "Hey. I like you. You're a great guy, and I didn't rule anything out with us."

The music starts to play, and we're interrupted before I get a response. Raising my hand, I feel my forehead. I'm making a bigger mess of things rather than fixing the damage.

My thoughts are interrupted when my father walks to the front of the aisle. He looks dapper in his deep red suit. Bouncing back and forth on his feet, he checks his watch. "I'm sure she'll be along any minute." He laughs nervously. It's cute to see him like this.

We don't have to wait long before the music changes and my mum gracefully walks to join him before the song fades out. The gorgeous ruby red dress she's picked out looks even better than in the shop. Her hair's curled, and the outfit is finished off with silver jewellery. "Don't look so tense, dear. You haven't forgotten I've already married you, have you?" Mum says, making everyone laugh. Even Archie cracks a smile.

A lady from the chairs at the front stands with my parents. She's dressed in an evergreen dress with red lipstick. Her inspiration seems to have come from a holly wreath. It wouldn't work for everyone, yet it does for her. She fits the Christmas theme with her outfit, and everything is looking fabulous for my parents.

"Welcome, ladies and gentlemen. My name's Eve and we're gathered here to celebrate the marriage of Edith and Martin Ainsworth," the woman says, making everyone cheer. "Each of them has written their own vows and are ready to share their love with us." She continues to talk about the value of marriage.

We watch my parents declare their devotion to each other, sharing a few treasured memories. Mum talks about how they met through her father, and Dad talks about how lovely he thought she was. Seeing them happy brings a tear to my eye. It's beautiful to see two people committed the way my parents are.

As soon as the ceremony is over, Archie's out of his chair and racing away from me. My stomach sinks. Bloody hell. I'm making him unhappy, which isn't what I wanted.

I follow him outside and towards the lodge. When I catch up with him, he's already in our bedroom.

No. No. No. I don't want him to walk out on me. My heart feels funny in my chest. "I can't do this anymore," he says, undoing his shirt.

"Why? What's wrong?" I close the door behind us, partially so we're not interrupted, but also to shut the rest of the world out. It's me and him. I need him to stay.

He moves to his bag and my fears come true. I grab hold of the handle, forcing him to look at me. He holds eye contact. "I'll transfer your five thousand pounds back into your account. I'm going home."

"The money is yours, but I want you to reconsider." I tighten my hand on the handle. I can't force him to give me another chance, but he will listen to me first.

He wavers for a second before putting his clothes into the bag. "I have feelings for you, which I didn't expect. I'm finding it hard to be around you." He pulls out a gift. "I was going to give you this tomorrow, but you can have it now."

I open it as he packs up the rest of his things. It's a beautiful travel planner. "Thank you." It's a thoughtful gift and it's perfect for me. Although, if he leaves, I'm not sure I could use it. It would remind me of what I've lost.

"I've seen a change in you over these last few days. I think you should consider taking more time out from your busy schedule."

He's correct. I am different. Partially because of him, but also because of my family. My eyes have been opened, and I don't want to go back to the way things were. This week has changed things, and I want to spend more time away from work.

He goes back to taking off the suit my brother hired for him. "I'm glad you've found what you were looking for."

I put my hand on his bare chest. It's firm but warm. I want to snuggle into him. Tears cloud my vision and I fight to hold them in. "Just stop and talk to me."

"What's left to say?" He stiffens but doesn't move away.

"Why are you leaving?" He's not making any sense. He said he liked me. We need to talk, not put distance between us.

"Because I like you, and coming here was a mistake."

This holiday has been one of the best. Not because I started to mend things with my family, although that's a bonus. It's him. He's special to me. I want to see him as much as I can. My mouth starts to get dry, but I force out the words. "I like you too and I don't want you to leave."

"Prove it." He puts his hands on his hips.

We stare at each other. I need to get this right or I'm going to lose him. "I want you to stay. Not because I'm paying you or you want to work with me. I want you to stay because we have a connection."

"I didn't mean with words." His arms flop to his side.

Stretching up onto my tiptoes, I press my lips to his. He doesn't react at first, so I kiss along his jawline to his neck before returning to his mouth. My hands find their way up his torso and down his back. "Do you want me to stop?" I ask.

"I don't want us to start something if you're going to regret it as soon as it's over."

"That's not why I pulled away. We'd been drinking and I value you too much to make a rash decision. I haven't dated in a long time, and I didn't want to get it wrong. I never meant to hurt your feelings. You're an amazing person. The last thing I wanted was to push you away."

"Why didn't you just talk to me the next morning?"

"My ex cheated on me in school, and I've never dated anyone I could see a future with after that." Alexander was the guy my parents picked out for me by the end of my A-levels, but Benedict was my first love. I didn't know how I was going to recover when he broke my heart. Admitting that out loud is like a weight off my chest. Archie is a man, not a high school boy. He's kind and caring. I have faith he won't hurt me.

He rubs my shoulders. "I'm not him."

"You've shown me that." I kiss his cheek. His hands go to my ass and he cups it, pulling me towards him. We flop down onto the bed and stare into each other's eyes.

"Tell me what you want." He strokes my hair, which sends tingles down my spine.

I kiss his lips softly, and he reciprocates this time. My hand caresses the hard skin on his chest, and I deepen the kiss. "I'd love to stay like this all day, but people will notice we're missing," I say.

"As long as you're not running, I'm happy to continue this later."

"I'm done running from you."

"Okay. Let's get back before people start to talk about us being gone." He kisses me one last time before we get to our feet. We make ourselves decent and go back to the celebration. Everyone looks wrapped up in their own love story when we return. Friends and family are talking. People are hugging, and there's a happy vibe. Now Archie seems happy, everything is perfect. We sit down to enjoy another hog roast meal.

"There's something magical about Christmas and weddings," I say, touching the scattered snowflake confetti on the table.

"I agree. This time next year, I'd be happy to repeat this whole experience," Archie says.

A sense of love washes over me. "Yes. That would be amazing. I want to spend next year with you. Plus, I'm going to stop avoiding family holidays. If we're lucky, we might be somewhere warmer next time."

"I'll pack a Santa hat and a Speedo next time." He chuckles to himself.

I nod. "I like that vision."

"I'll get you a hat too."

"Sounds great." I smile brightly.

We enjoy the food, and after dessert, Archie stands, offering me his hand. "Dance with me."

"It would be my pleasure." I take his hand and we walk onto the dance floor.

He wraps his arms around my waist, and I nestle against his chest for a slow song. He smells so good. It's like a woodsy smell with a hint of cinnamon. "Will you let me take you out dancing for New Year?"

"You're a great dancer. That sounds like fun." We sway to the music.

"I'm going to show you all the things I'm good at." He winks at me, and my cheeks burn.

"I already said I like kissing you." A vision of him on top of me in the bedroom sends a wave of pleasure through me.

He laughs. "I meant organising dates for us to enjoy."

"Oh," I say, biting my lip. As I begin to smirk, I look away. That wasn't the idea I'd had. I've already seen him almost naked. The rest of him is probably just as nice.

Archie gently lifts my chin. "I like your train of thought, though." He kisses my lips as heat travels up my face.

"I'm a little embarrassed." I cover my mouth, feeling naughty for having lustful thoughts.

"Don't be. It's just me and you." We kiss again.

We dance together for the next few songs until my dad interrupts us. "Do you mind if I cut in?" he asks.

"Be my guest," Archie says, offering my arm.

"It was a beautiful ceremony," I say once Archie retreats to the table.

"Yes. Your mother did a great job." We dance the basic two-step pattern. My dad was the one who taught me it when I was younger.

"Have you enjoyed the day?"

"Yes. What will make my Christmas complete is for my daughter to forgive me for thinking I knew what was best for her future."

I miss a step, and my dad almost collides into me. A tear slips down my face. It's been an emotional day and I can't fight it any longer. "I forgive you, Dad. I love you so much."

He wipes away my tears before pulling me into a hug. "Don't cry or you'll set me off. I love you too."

"Thank you. Today has given me the best presents I could've asked for." We hug some more.

"Promise me you'll make more time for your mother and me."

"I promise." We finish the dance and then he kisses my cheek before I go back to Archie.

"After seeing you glide around the dancefloor with your dad, I think you lied to me about thinking I'm a good dancer," Archie says.

I sit next to him. "I can show you the two-step moves if you'd like, but I prefer holding you closer."

"Do you think it's too early to slip back out?" He smiles.

"Just so I don't get myself flustered again, do you mean what I think you mean?"

He smirks. "Let's start with this." He takes my hand and leads me to the doorway. It's almost Christmas, and we kiss passionately under the mistletoe.

"This is very romantic." I kiss him again.

"I thought you were one of those people who didn't show public affection," Charles says as he passes us.

With anyone else, that would be true. With Archie, I want to go with the flow. "You're just jealous you don't have a special man," I tease.

"Yes. I am." Charles shrugs.

"We'll find you a Londoner so you'll have to stay close to home," Archie says.

"I like the sound of that," Charlies replies with a huge smile. I can already imagine them gaming on my sofa. Archie has easily become part of my life, and I like it.

I'd love to see more of my brother too.

We say our goodbyes to everyone before making our way back to the lodge. Everyone's at the party and we have the place to ourselves. We take it in turns to use the bathroom. I remove my make-up and change into my silky black nightie. Archie's seen me like this every night since we came to the Winter Lodges.

Once Archie's stripped down to just his boxers, we climb into bed. "Should I turn the light off?" I ask.

"Only if you'd like to," Archie says, stroking the side of my face.

"No. I want to see you." My hands wrap around his shoulders, and I pull him into a kiss. This time, I don't hold anything back. My moans are loud as we kiss like we can't get enough. I massage down his back as I explore his skin. He pulls down my nightie strap so he can kiss along my collarbone. I indulge in the smell of his soft, clean hair. It's smells of orange and eucalyptus, mixed with a hint of cinnamon.

The smooth silk of my nightie moves up my thigh. Heat spreads up my body, but this time, it's not from embarrassment. My pussy slickens and my nipples harden. I grind against Archie, feeling his hard length. This is actually happening, and I don't want to ruin it by overthinking, but he's going to see me naked.

His kisses a trail down onto my bust as he moves the fabric lower. The soft sensation mixed with the heat of his mouth brings my body to life. Slowly, I stroke along the waistline of his boxers while my lips make their way over the back of his shoulder.

He grips the hem of my nightie, squeezing the inside of my leg. His hands move closer to my intimate area, and the anticipation is killing me. I push my hands into the back of his boxers, grabbing a handful of his lush ass. He moves his kisses to my lips so he can wrap his legs around mine. There's no denying the bulge in his pants is huge.

I edge down his boxers until his dick springs loose, and he lifts my nightdress, exposing my pussy. We stop kissing, and he brings my nightie over my head, letting it fall to the floor. We stare into each other's eyes for a few seconds.

"I've wanted you since we first met," Archie whispers.

I smile. It's nice to feel desired. "I've never been so turned on."

We kiss again. "I'm about to find out." His finger barely touches my clit as he teases me.

I let out a frustrated moan. "You don't play fair."

"You've taught me the art of taking it slow." He smiles. I guess he's been sexually frustrated since our misfire the other night.

Hastily, I reach down and take hold of his dick. I squeeze the shaft before beginning to stroke the length. Archie lets out a low-pitched moan, giving me my first glimpse of satisfaction. "We've done enough waiting. I want you now."

He bites his lip seductively as he dips his finger into

my pussy. I close my eyes, loving the sensation. His fingers move over my clit, and he circles my sweet spot. "You're so wet." I stroke his dick faster, and he quickens his hand movements.

"Do you have a condom?" I ask.

"Yes," he says in a gravelly voice. He kisses me one more time before going to retrieve it. He opens the packet and slips the condom onto his length. He removes his boxer shorts. I lie down on the bed and he climbs on top, positioning himself at my entrance. "Are you ready?"

I nod. "Yes."

He pushes inside me, stretching me, making me feel full. He waits for me to adjust before pulling out and thrusting back inside. I've missed sex. It's been so long, and I'd forgotten how good it can feel.

With every thrust, I feel like I've gone to heaven. I wrap my legs around his waist, deepening our connection.

"You feel so good." He caresses my body until his hand rests on my hip.

"You're amazing."

"No, you're the incredible one." We kiss again. He continues to move in and out of me. His pace quickens, bringing me closer to the edge. My body feels hot everywhere, and the pleasure intensifies in my core. I can't hold in my moan any longer. I orgasm loudly, letting go of all my inhibitions. Archie pushes deeper and faster until he lets out his own moan. He comes with a satisfied grunt before collapsing on top of me.

"That was fun," he says in between erratic breaths.

"Yes, it was." I kiss his shoulder.

"Maybe we should do it again sometime." He strokes my hair affectionately.

"More than once." I run my fingers down his arm, loving the sensation of his soft skin.

"That sounds like a great idea." He leans in and softly kisses my lips. "Merry Christmas, Victoria."

"Merry Christmas, Archie."

Santa brought me exactly what I needed this year. A friend, a lover, and my family. I'm looking forward to the future and seeing where things go with dating my new man.

CHAPTER THIRTEEN

After last night's party, I'm slow to get going on Christmas Day. I pull the duvet up to my chin and hold on to the idea of staying in bed.

"Morning beautiful," Archie says as he turns to face me.

A warm blush creeps up my face as I remember the sex we had when we were finally alone last night. "Good morning," I say.

"Do you think he's been yet?" Archie asks in an excited voice.

"Santa might've brought you something, but so have I." Leaning out of the bed, I retrieve the paper bag I got from my trip into town and hand it to Archie.

"Thank you." He opens it, pulling out a t-shirt that says *#1 boyfriend*. He laughs. "This is awesome."

"I bought it before I realised how much I liked you, and it was supposed to be a joke." It cost ten pounds, and I wish I'd put more thought into his gift.

"I'm going to get your name added to the bottom." He points to the space under the writing.

"Does that mean we're making our relationship official?" I'm nervous about his answer, but I want Archie to be my boyfriend. Spending time with him feels so right, and I can't picture him anywhere but at my side.

"From the second we met, I knew you'd be mine," he says smugly, and I relax. He's so good at reassuring me at the right time.

"That's a bold statement. How could you have known?" I bite my lip. His confidence in me has never wavered. He's had high expectations of me doing the right thing, and in the end, he was right.

"When we met, you were looking at me like I was a tasty snack, and then you chose the choir boy. There had to be a reason why you made that crazy decision." He shakes his head, frowning at me disapprovingly.

"That's what I said to Melanie. He did look like a choir boy."

He laughs. "Then why make a stupid mistake?"

"Because you reminded me of my high school boyfriend. Not the way you look. It was your energy. I judged you unfairly. I thought you were a heartbreaker because he was. Now I know differently. Archibald Banks is a keeper."

He moves to the edge of the bed and retrieves a small box. "I got you a small gift."

"I thought I'd already had my present." I poke my finger into the seal.

"I'm allowed to get you two."

I open the box and find a necklace from Zosie. "When did you get this?" It's a silver chain with a charm that looks like a fabric cutting.

"I ordered it the day after the photoshoot. Do you like it?"

Wow. He really was confident he'd get a chance to give it to me. "I love it."

My knees feel weak as my heart fills with love or something close. We kiss. It's soft and sensual. I care for this man and he makes me feel alive in a way I never thought possible. Archie is wonderful, and the gift is perfect. With every step he takes, showing me he cares, I'm falling that little bit more. I'm completely smitten.

Santa has brought each of my family members and Archie several gifts. We sit in the living room while my mum cooks Christmas dinner.

"Aww, we have matching jumpers," Charles says, holding his ugly snowman jumper up to Archie.

"We can wear them next Christmas," Archie says. They both laugh like the idea is hysterical. I shake my head.

"I can join in too," my dad says, holding up his own jumper. They all cheer.

It's so nice to see the men in my life happy about matching. Next year's Christmas card is going to be unfashionable, and I love it. I'm handed a present from my aunt and find my own woolly snowman jumper.

"Wahoo," Charles says, eyeing it up.

Holding it up to my chest, I show it off.

"Dinner is ready," Mum says, and we move to the table. The food is passed around, and I help myself to a bit of everything.

"Thanks, Mum," I say.

A chorus of thank yous echoes around the table.

"I'm glad to have my family here. Merry Christmas." Mum holds her glass up and we all say *cheers*.

After eating, Charles and Archie play FIFA. My dad takes a walk, and my aunt disappears to her room. I help Mum wash up.

"It's not quite New Year, but I want you to know my resolution will be to work less and enjoy life more," I say.

"I'm proud of you," my mum says, kissing my head.

"You could've told me you wanted me to focus less on my work."

"I tried. I'm sorry I didn't handle it better. I want to spend more time with you when we get back to London."

"I'd like that too." We hug before turning back to the dishes.

After cleaning up and sitting with my family for a while, Archie and I decide to go for a walk. I hold my hand out and a drop of snow lands in my palm. "It's snowing." I state the obvious.

"It's the perfect ending to a perfect Christmas," Archie says, putting his arm around my shoulders.

"Indeed it is." We kiss before joining hands and walking into the night.

CHAPTER FOURTEEN

"You seem chipper," Melanie says as she enters my office. She puts my cup of tea on the table. It's the first day back in the office after the winter break.

I stop humming and dancing to the radio. "I am. How was your winter break?" I ask.

She laughs. "Trust you to skip over the main events. I had a great Christmas and the kids got everything they wanted from Santa. Did you get anything good? Have you redesigned the spring collection?" She laughs. Usually, she'd be right. I have made a change to my schedule, though.

"I haven't had a chance to look at my sketchbook. I've been busy," I say cryptically with a light shrug of my shoulders.

She takes a seat and leans on the table. "Ooh, do tell." I've missed my assistant's enthusiasm.

"I spent my holiday in Cornwall with my family." I sit down too, giving her my full attention.

She clutches her hand to her chest. "Aww, I love a heart-warming Christmas. Did you make beautiful memories?"

"I did. My parents renewed their vows." I've already agreed to a holiday at the Winter Lodges next December.

Melanie is swooning all over this story. She's a true romantic and it's cute. "I bet that was amazing against the Cornish and Christmas backdrop."

"It was perfect for them. My parents looked so happy. The break away from normal life was good for everyone."

"Is that the only reason you're so vibrant today?" She eyes me curiously.

"I took Archie with me to the Winter Lodges." I bite my lip, waiting for her reaction.

She clicks her fingers and points at me. "I knew he was special."

I give a knowing smile. "Me too."

"Tell me everything."

I give her the details about my original rent-a-date and how our relationship blossomed. Instead of working, we talk about our Christmas break over a couple of cups of tea.

There's a knock on my office door, and Archie comes into my office. He kisses my cheek. "Hello, ladies."

"Hello, Archie. It's great to see you here again," Melanie says. Her smile is so wide I can't help mirroring it.

"Archie's going to help us with the material samples for the boyfriend collection."

"I'm so excited to see what you've come up with." She grabs a pencil, ready to take notes.

"Actually, I value your opinion, and I thought we could all work on this together. Victoria Ainsworth is no longer a one-woman team."

The atmosphere in my office is amazing as we look at fabrics together. I have the best job in the world, and I'm realising I need my whole team.

After a great day, Archie and I walk through the streets of London. "Thank you for including me in your boyfriend collection," he says.

"It was a no-brainer. Whoever said you can't mix business with pleasure hadn't met you." We hold hands, and I'm proud to have him by my side. He's more than just my new boyfriend. He's the missing piece from my life.

"Rent-a-date might be my legacy. I should start a website." He squeezes my hand comfortingly.

"Swipe right for a perfect date?" I'm unsure if Archie

is being serious, but I'd support a business like that. If we hadn't gone to that ball, we might've never made it to this day.

"If I match models and fashion designers, and hotel managers with interior designers, I might get a new nickname."

I kiss his cheek. "Doctor Love?"

"No." He shakes his head. "The design fixer, or the meet cute perfecter."

"We can work on the nickname, but I like the principle of it. Come on, Mr Fixer. Let's get you home." We walk to my apartment, throwing ideas back and forth.

Once we reach my front door, I unlock it and we go inside. We have one rule when it comes to our free time together; no work at the end of the day, although Archie's business idea is hard to shake. Together, we make risotto, and we sit down with a glass of wine. "To us," Archie says, holding up his glass.

"To the future of us."

I have a good feeling about this year. We're only in the early days of our official relationship, but we already have plans. We have the boyfriend collection, a meal with my parents when they return from the Bahamas, and a date at the theatre. Being with Archie feels right, and who knows what our next adventure will be?

EPILOGUE
Archie

I tug on the fitted royal blue suit jacket Victoria made me while staring in the full-length mirror. "It's gorgeous, just like you," I say.

Victoria comes to stand behind me. "You look good enough to date."

I laugh. "So, you're dressing me up so I'm respectable?"

"Absolutely not. If it was up to me, we'd be naked in bed together." I turn around to kiss her.

"We'll both be late if we get back between the sheets." She pulls on my jacket then brings me back to her lips.

"It would be worth it."

"Don't tempt me." Slowly, our lips meet, and we kiss softly at first, but it quickly deepens into a passionate make-out. We've lived together for a few months now, and this never gets old. My watch beeps, signalling we're going to be late.

She straightens my shirt. "It's time to go."

I touch the necklace I bought her last Christmas. "Good luck with your interview today."

She smiles. "Thanks." Rebel Jacks is starting a sister company, Revolution Jacks. Victoria has the vision to run the branch, and today is the day she'll pitch her idea.

We collect our work things and exit the apartment. I help her load her things into the car before we set off. We hold hands on the back seat as the driver takes us to Rebel Jacks first.

"I'll see you at lunch," I say when we arrive.

"Yes. Either with a bottle of wine to celebrate or some port to drown my sorrows." She pretends to cry before gritting her teeth.

"Don't be nervous. You've got this."

"I got this," she repeats, trying to up her positivity. We kiss goodbye and then the driver drops me at Baker Street.

The black door of my office looks just like any other, but my business holds a secret. I unlock the door and step inside.

Everything in this building, including my clothes, were picked by my girlfriend. Some of my modelling pictures line the walls, and the embossed flowered wallpaper makes the space look very chic.

I open up the studio room and unlock my office. I'm not waiting long until someone enters. "Are you lost or looking for modelling work?" I ask.

"I'm lost in love," the young woman says, explaining why she's here. Her honey blonde hair and striking blue eyes are familiar.

"Welcome to Rent-A-Date where we find your step-in boyfriends," I say as she hurries away from the outside world. I follow her down the hall towards the door marked out for my special clients. She has inside information or she wouldn't know where to go. I've seen her somewhere before, but I haven't quite put the pieces together yet.

My discreet location is only available to those who need me. Either through word of mouth or an encoded website. Everyone else thinks this is a modelling studio, and it is on Tuesdays and Thursdays.

She looks over her shoulder to check nobody other than me is following her. "Is it safe for us to talk freely? I don't want anyone to know I'm here." She's not the first client to value her privacy and I'm already intrigued as to what kind of date she needs.

"We take confidentially very seriously at Rent-A-Date. Please take a seat and I'll lock the door." I gesture to the chair in my office. I've been running my business for five months now and I know when to lock the outside door. I walk back down the hall and secure my building. My receptionist won't be in for another couple of hours so it's just the two of us.

When I return, she's still hesitating in the middle of the room. "Get comfortable. We won't be disturbed." I point at the chair once more.

"Thank you." She takes a seat in a purple velvet armchair, and I secure the office door so she understands it's just us.

"I'm Archibald Banks, the founder of Rent-A-Date. How can I help you, Miss…"

"Jones, or you can call me Faith."

"How can I help you, Miss Faith Jones?" Now, that's a name I recognise, but I try not to let it show. She's the heiress of songwriter Ralf Jones.

She leans forward. "I need more than a date. I'm looking for a serious boyfriend."

This might lead to a high-profile date, but we can handle anything. "I have a number of charming guys who would love to meet your needs. When do you want them to start?" I begin mentally looking through possible matches. The guy will need to be used to fame but not too close to the spotlight. *A photographer or music producer maybe?*

"We need to make it look like we're in love." She's still whispering, and I don't understand why.

"Wait. Go back a step. Are you wanting a long-term boyfriend?" I've not done a fake setup on this kind of scale before. It can be done, though. I'm sure I can entice Victoria to help. Their backstory needs to be strong to avoid suspicion. What are the chances you'd have a serious relationship with someone your family and friends have never met? My thoughts go back to the present as I wait for Faith to continue.

"I'm wanting someone that will commit to being with me and nobody else. He'd have to live with me." She holds eye contact.

I stare at her for a few seconds, searching for any signs she's joking. She keeps a serious face. "You know Rent-a-date is a fake dating agency, right?"

"Yes. I'm not interested in falling in love or having a relationship, but I need a man."

A date for a night is completely different to what Faith is asking for. "Why is this important to you?"

"If I want to inherit my family's fortune, I have to show I'm responsible, even though I'm perfectly content being on my own." She bites her lip.

"You're an attractive woman. Why don't you already have a guy in your life you can ask?"

"I'm too busy with work, and I'm not looking to complicate a relationship." I glance at the picture of my Victoria, which is on my desk. She didn't think she needed someone either. Maybe I can help Faith in more ways than she thinks.

"I can help you if you trust my decisions." If we don't want this to blow up in her face, we'll need to lay down some rules. The boyfriend she wants will need to be inserted into all aspects of her life. She won't be able to hide from him or people will know their relationship isn't real. If the guy I choose can pull this off, this might be my greatest success, and if they find love, it'll be a bonus. I'm not that kind of matchmaker, though. I'll find her a guy that can play the role over what she finds attractive.

"You were recommended to me by my PA's friend. She knows your girlfriend's assistant, Melanie. I do have some questions, though."

This is starting to make more sense now. "Please go ahead."

"What qualifies you to find the perfect man for the job? Do you have any testimonies?"

"I do, but for obvious reasons, they're anonymous." Pulling some laminated sheets from the top drawer of my desk, I hand them over.

She reads over them. "Do you have a client I can talk to?"

"I'm sorry, I don't, but if you give me a chance to find what you're looking for, I can introduce you and you can see what you think."

She looks at the sheet again. "Okay. Let's see who you come up with."

I'm excited to take on Faith, and I'm confident I'll find her the perfect boyfriend. "I'll make us some coffee and we'll get to work." I start preparing to take

Faith's details so I can match her personality to the right guy.

"Coffee would be good. I like you already, Archie." She smiles, finally leaning back in the chair.

"You're going to love your new partner even more."

I make the drinks, and we sit down with the questionnaire I've put together. Once I'm happy I've got everything I need, we say our goodbyes and she leaves. I sit at my desk, looking through the database I've created on potential matches.

A little after noon, Victoria arrives with a large gift basket. She puts it down on my desk and kisses my cheek. "Hello. I brought wine and cheese."

"Hello." I quickly switch off the laptop. "Don't leave me in suspense. How did it go?"

"I got the job." She holds her hands out to me.

I stand up and spin her around. "I knew you would." I couldn't be prouder. I love this beautiful woman more than anything. "I love you."

"I love you too. Thanks for having the confidence in me." We hug and kiss some more. "How did your morning go?"

"I have a potential new client."

"Ooh, that's exciting."

"Let's get some lunch and I'll tell you all about it," I say.

Victoria has changed my life, and everything has fallen into place perfectly. I know she's the woman I want to spend the rest of my life with. I'm just waiting for the right moment to tell her. The simple things like grabbing lunch are so much better now it's the two of us.

The End

ABOUT THE AUTHOR

Danielle lives in Yorkshire, England, with her husband, daughter, and tortoise. She enjoys reading, watching the rain, and listening to old music. Her dreams include writing stories, visiting magical places, and staying young at heart. The people who know her describe her as someone who has her head in the clouds and her mind in a book.

Danielle is a multi-genre author with a love for all things romance. Her most successful book is the Kiss & Tell: an Amaryllis Media anthology which was a best seller across two platforms. Danielle enjoys world building and creating unbreakable bonds.

ACKNOWLEDGEMENTS

When the idea for Rent-a-date anthology was first pitched, I already had a love for fake dating. Dirty Kisses and Conflicting Wishes was so much fun to write, so I knew I had to do this. The idea of Victoria came to me, and I wanted to give this headstrong woman what she deserved. I hope you enjoy the world I created for her and the man she loves.

When writing a story, the first draft is the pages that aren't seen by many. With the help of my beta team and Karen Sanders, my editor, this story has really come to life. I can't thank any of you enough.

Melanie is the person who gets my early drafts, and we talk about the characters like they are real people. By the time this has worked its way to Jackie, Rebecca, Mich, and Yvonne it's beginning to take shape. Thank you for helping me add the sparkle.

Karen Sanders has done an absolutely amazing job editing this story and I'll never be able to thank her enough for everything she does. From the support to helping my dreams become reality.

Last but not least, thank you J.E. Feldman for allowing me to join the anthology and starting my obsession with Archie.

What started as a standalone may become more.

Connect with Danielle Jacks

https://danielle-jacks-author.mailchimpsites.com/

Read other books by Danielle Jacks

The Heart of Baker Bay

Kickflip Summer

Dirty Kisses and Conflicting Wishes

Burned by Fire

Confessions of a Sophomore Prankster

Romance Under Aquarius

Twisted Bond